Renegade Boys

MEESHA

Lock Down Publications and Ca$h
Presents
Renegade Boys
A Novel by *Meesha*

Lock Down Publications
P.O. Box 870494
Mesquite, Tx 75187

Visit our website @
www.lockdownpublications.com

Copyright 2018 Renegade Boys

First Edition November 2018
Printed in the United States of America

This is a work of fiction. Names, characters, places, and incidents either are products of the author's imagination or are used fictitiously. Any similarity to actual events or locales or persons, living or dead, is entirely coincidental.

Lock Down Publications
Like our page on Facebook: Lock Down Publications @
www.facebook.com/lockdownpublications.ldp
Cover design and layout by: **Dynasty Cover Me**
Book interior design by: **Shawn Walker**
Edited by: **Tam Jernigan**

Stay Connected with Us!

Text **LOCKDOWN** to 22828 to stay up-to-date with new releases, sneak peaks, contests and more…
Or **CLICK HERE** to sign up.
Thank you.

Like our page on Facebook:

Lock Down Publications: Facebook

Join Lock Down Publications/The New Era Reading Group

Visit our website @ www.lockdownpublications.com

Follow us on Instagram:

Lock Down Publications: Instagram

Email Us: We want to hear from you!

Submission Guideline.

Submit the first three chapters of your completed manuscript to ldpsubmissions@gmail.com, subject line: Your book's title. The manuscript must be in a .doc file and sent as an attachment. Document should be in Times New Roman, double spaced and in size 12 font. Also, provide your synopsis and full contact information. If sending multiple submissions, they must each be in a separate email.

Have a story but no way to send it electronically? You can still submit to LDP/Ca$h Presents. Send in the first three chapters, written or typed, of your completed manuscript to:

LDP: Submissions Dept
Po Box 870494
Mesquite, Tx 75187

DO NOT send original manuscript. Must be a duplicate.

Provide your synopsis and a cover letter containing your full contact information.

Thanks for considering LDP and Ca$h Presents.

Dedications

I want to dedicate this book to my publisher Ca$h. This man literally gave me the opportunity to showcase my craft and he believed in me when I didn't believe in myself. The motivational conversations that we had were exactly what I needed when I didn't think I was doing good with my writing.

With his great wisdom and knowledge of the industry, Ca$h paved the way for me to strive. When I signed the contract to join the Lockdown Publication family, I didn't know what I was getting into. I can honestly say, I wouldn't change anything about my decision.

Bossman, I want you to know that I appreciate you and Shawn so much. The growth that I see in my writing comes from the encouraging words from you two. Thank you.

The world is ours when it comes to LDP! Congratulations again on your release! It's been a month and some change and there's great things in store for you, Bossman. Take everything day by day and things will come together as they may. Your second chance will be the best one for you...I'm claiming it!

I can't thank you enough for believing in me. This book goes hard and I hope I make you proud with it. Ca$h you are appreciated, THANK YOU!

MEESHA

Chapter 1
Mauricio

Pulling up to the trap that I ran on 26th street, I cut the engine. The bass that boomed from the trap could be heard from inside my ride. It didn't look like these mufuckas were selling dope, in fact I knew they weren't. There wasn't one nigga outside for the crackheads to buy shit from. As I got out the car, a fiend rushed up to me.

"Yo, my man, can I get three blows from you? I've been waiting out here for the longest and no one is answering the door."

Hearing him say that pissed me off because I knew money wasn't being made. I went back to my car and grabbed the three rocks he asked for and gave him his medicine. He hurried off fast looking over his shoulder. I took a deep breath before I walked toward the crib slowly trying to control my anger.

I turned the knob hoping and praying it was locked, but it wasn't. There was nothing that could stop the rage that was ripping through my bloodstream at that moment. I walked in and there was a full-blown sex session taking place. These fools had bitches, drinks, loud, and the music turned up to the max. Mell was in the corner getting his shit wet with his eyes closed and his mouth hanging open. The broad that was polishing his knob was giving his stupid ass the business because he was oblivious that I was there.

Lil Jay was sitting on the sofa with two bitches sucking his dick and balls, with his eyes closed. Sergio and Rico were having a threesome with a thick bitch in the corner. One was fucking her viciously, while the other massaged her scalp as she swallowed his tool.

There were several more of my workers that were getting it on with bitches in different parts of the room. There was one big ass orgy taking place on my dime. I walked quietly to the back of the house where there were three bedrooms. The party continued back there as well. I told these knuckleheads to come to this trap for a meeting, but they were disrespecting my shit to the fullest. Not only that, I could've been any damn body that walked in there.

"Get the fuck up and get to the front of this mufucka! Y'all got a lot of fuckin' nerve!" I yelled walking out repeating the shit in the other bedrooms. Walking back to the front of the house, them niggas still didn't know I was walking through that bitch. I couldn't stand there another minute watching these stupid idiots do they thang.

Walking over to the stereo, I turned the music off. Not one person stopped what the fuck they were doing. It was a damn shame I had to make my presence known. They should've been alert at all times. "What the fuck you niggas on?" With the sound of my voice, everyone started scrambling around like roaches trying to find clothes and covering up their bodies. "I've been here for well over ten minutes and not one of y'all knew I was here! This ain't no damn brothel, get these bitches out of here! All of you mufuckas done lost ya minds! I'm six four, two sixty-five, a big mufucka and y'all didn't see my ass when I entered! Anybody could've walked in here and murked all you dummies and my money would've walked out with them. This is the reason I tell y'all I don't want no damn body in my shit! But you niggas don't listen!"

The four muthafuckas and their hoes came from the back looking stupid as fuck. I gave each of them the look of death and the females were taking their walk of shame with their heads down. *If they were going to trick the fuck off, they needed to learn to wear that shit with pride.* I thought to myself. Lil Jay broke into my thoughts when he opened his mouth.

"Ricio—," Lil Jay tried to speak, but I cut his ass right off.

"Shut the fuck up! I don't want to hear shit!" I looked around and noticed the females were dressed. "You hoes can bounce, y'all gargled enough babies around this bitch for one night, get the fuck out."

"Who you calling a hoe, nigga? Yo' mama's a hoe, bitch!"

At that moment everybody paused. Shawty fucked up when she let that slick shit slide out her throat. She couldn't have known that I didn't take disrespect lightly. Her being a female didn't give her a pass by any means.

Looking shawty up and down, I had to do a double take. She was stacked in all the right places and was cute as hell. I loved me a redbone, but her mouthpiece made her ugly as fuck. On top of that, she called my mama a hoe and my OG was chillin' with my Pops and the Man Upstairs. I pulled my .44 from behind my back and shot that bitch right between her eyes. *Boc*! Her body appeared to fall in slow motion, but her head burst open like a watermelon slapping the concrete.

One of the females let out a shrieking cry but I didn't give a fuck. I had no remorse for what I had done. "I don't give a fuck who you are, if you disrespect me, I have no words for you at all. But there will be some hot shit that will burn the shit out ya ass. This ain't the Bunny Ranch and don't none of you niggas look like Hugh Hefner. If turning up is what you want to do, so be it. Do it on yo' own time. This is a business, not a playground. Let me know if you can't handle it and you can leave when the ladies leave, won't be no coming back! Don't think none of y'all are irreplaceable, because I can find some hungry lil niggas out there in the streets that want to get this money that y'all been passing up for hours. I shouldn't have to come over here to serve fiends, that's what y'all here for!"

"You didn't have to kill her, Ricio." Lil Jay cried out.

I glanced in his direction and wanted to slap his pussy ass. He was crying legit real tears over that wannabe gangsta ass bitch. He should've told her how the fuck I rolled and maybe she'd still be breathing. "Fuck you and yo' punk ass tears, Jay! You should've trained that bitch to keep her damn mouth closed. But since you love her so much, go join that hoe."

Boc! I shot him straight through the heart and didn't even watch to see where his body landed. Glancing around the room I noticed no one moved a muscle. It was like they were in the middle of a game of red light, green light and they were forced to freeze in place.

"I'm gon' say this one time and one time only. Y'all don't know shit and ya ain't seen shit. Once you leave this mufucka, twelve bet not show up. If I have any heat around my establishment, I'll be to see you and ya whole family. That goes for every last one of y'all, now get the fuck out!"

As the last female left the trap, the only thing I could do was shake my head. This temper of mine had to be checked. Nobody could deny that it had become a problem. I called the cleanup crew to come clean up the mess I had made.

"Yo, the kitchen sink is leaking in apartment A, there's a toilet that's clogged too."

"Say less."

That was the code for two bodies so they would know what they were working with. Pacing the floor back and forth, I was frustrated. These young niggas gon' make me go postal. I'm tired of having to preach to them about the importance of staying alert. They are going to get serious about this shit or come up missing, simple as that. Floyd was always on my ass about them slacking, I was tired of him coming at me because of their bullshit.

"Now that I can conduct business, make this my first and last time coming to my place of business and there's bullshit like what I saw going down. That's not how the fuck I operate. The only occupants that should be in here are the people that work for me, no one else. If you ain't about money, you can leave this bitch, in a body bag." I said looking into the eyes of each of them.

Before I could continue talking, the sound of the special knock echoed through the house. "It's open!" I said with venom dripping off my lips.

My loyal niggas Sosa, Butta, Psycho, AK, Face, Felon, and Fats walked through the door. With all the shit that had gone on, I forgot I'd told them to meet me at the trap. We've all been rocking for years and Sosa was my brother. When my Pops died, Big Jim put us on and gave us our own spot to run. I brought all my niggas in with me. When I eat, they're damn sure going to eat with me. It's been the eight of us for the past four years and I trust them with my life.

"Damn, Ricio, what the fuck is this shit Sosa asked stepping over the bodies that were laid out on the floor.

"Brah, you know how it goes, I can't have nobody testing my mufuckin' gangsta! I don't give a fuck if it was a bitch. Somebody should've taught her ass the do's and don'ts of addressing a real nigga."

"Well what the fuck happened to Lil Jay?" Felon asked looking around at the faces of the scary niggas that I was lecturing minutes before.

"That nigga wanted to cry about me shooting his bitch, so I shot his ass so they could be together! Fuck you mean?"

Sosa glanced around the room after cutting his eyes at me, trying to scope out a nigga that would talk to him about what went down. He focused his attention on a nigga named Sergio.

"Aye, Sergio, what the hell went on in this muthafucka, fam? And don't lie either, I want the raw deal." Sosa said as he walked toward him.

"We had a couple bitches come through just to chill with for a minute, you know—"

Sosa was shaking his head the entire time he was talking like, 'nope nigga, you know that's a no no. All that could be seen was the fire in his eyes because like myself, he didn't like anyone messing with his cash flow. Sosa was the calm before the storm of the crew and he didn't like when niggas weren't about making money.

"So, y'all thought it was trill to have females in the trap? This girl's blood is on all y'all hands now. This shit could've been avoided. Why the fuck didn't y'all go to Adrianna's or some shit? The muthafuckin' trap isn't a place to play with ya dicks! It's a business and will be treated as such. Take this shit as a warning, my niggas, this is not the shit y'all want.

There were a bunch of 'my bad, and we understand' coming from all fifteen of them, but we needed to discuss business. I had too much money in the street for mufuckas to be sitting around scratching their asses thinking shit was sweet. They needed to get their heads in the game and keep it there.

"We got a shipment coming in three days, I'm gon' need all y'all to be on ya shit. There's no room for slackin'. Straight business and getting this money, ya feel me? Butta, Fats, AK, and Psycho will be at the warehouse as usual for the shipment. Face, and Felon, I want y'all at the Empire waiting for the others to come through for the drop-off. Sosa and I will come through and help get shit in order once we get confirmation that all is good. The rest of you mufuckas, be ready to fill ya traps to feed these fiend's appetites. Keep the phones on and be ready to roll, I'm not trying to hear no excuses. Let's get this money, meeting adjourned."

As the niggas that didn't work in that particular trap filed out, I was studying every last one of them for signs of deception. I didn't give a fuck about rockin' anybody to sleep if I thought they were disloyal. I hated a snake mufucka with a passion.

"Aye brah, let's step outside for a few so I can holla at you." Sosa said not waiting on a response as he stormed out the door.

I knew he was about to talk shit about what I had done. Shooting Lil jay and his bitch was overboard but I couldn't take the shit back now. Regret was something I didn't feel. Shit, in the last four years, I didn't possess any feelings at all.

"Mauricio, you are gon' have to calm the fuck down brah!" he said as soon as I stepped outside. You can't keep letting your trigger finger make the decisions for you. I know things has been hard since Pops and ma were taken away from us, I still feel that shit too. It will only draw unnecessary heat our way. Save that shit for the niggas in the streets. You have to learn to control yourself."

"I try to control my anger, Sosa! That shit is easier said than done! You weren't there to see papí get shot in the back of the fuckin' head, or ma laying on the kitchen floor with a needle sticking out her arm, I was! ¡Todavía tengo pesadillas sobre esa mierda! Entonces, no me digas cómo coño sentir! (I still have nightmares about that shit! So, don't tell me how the fuck to feel!)" When I was extremely upset, I tended to revert from English to Spanish.

"I'm not telling you how you should feel. All I'm saying is, you have to control yo' temper. What the fuck did you accomplish by killin' two muthafuckas, Ricio? Not shit! Getting locked the fuck up for murder is not gon' solve none of yo' problems. For you to be the oldest of us all, you have been making dumb ass mistakes for no reason, other than letting your frustrations out. Go to the gym and punch a bag or something. I'm not trying to be out here without you, brah."

"I can do what the fuck I want to do. Let me deal with shit my way."

"Aight, I tried. A hard head makes a soft ass, nigga. I won't say shit else about it."

"Good."

Sosa was always trying to be on that be cool ass shit, that ain't me no more. He already knows what type of person life turned me into. I wish he would see that shit for what it was and keep that rationing mentality for himself. I wasn't calming shit down until I found out what happened to my parents. I left his ass standing on the front lawn and got in my whip burning rubber.

Chapter 2
Sosa

I watched as Mauricio walked to his car and peeled off. Pissing him off was the last thing I wanted to do. His ass would fuck around and take his frustrations out on the first person that said something he didn't like. He wasn't always a loose cannon, but I was the only one that could calm him down somewhat since our parents passed away four years prior.

My brother's and I didn't choose the life that we lived, it was something that was forced upon us. My little brother Maximo and I were still considered minors when papí was killed and ma died. We were ordered to live with papí's right hand man, Big Jim. He had documentation signed by papí stating if anything should happen to them, that's who we would live with.

Reese, that was my papí, was the Kingpin of Chicago. He was feared and respected by everyone. The people in the communities appreciated him because although he sold drugs and kept the crackheads fed, he put just as much money into the neighborhoods. The Boys & Girls Club on the Southside, the basketball camp on the Northside, and the many homeless shelters around the city were funded by Maurice Williams, better known as Reese.

He had police lieutenants, politicians, judges, and prosecutors on his payroll so he was untouchable. He had a loving wife and his three sons that he took care of. So, for him to be setup and killed didn't sit well with me. Of course, there were plenty of niggas that hated on him, but there wasn't anyone dumb enough to come at him in that way. I believed it was an inside job but didn't have proof, but what happened in the dark always comes to light.

Mauricio went to School at the *University of Chicago* he got his degree in business because he made that promise to our parents. I was currently in my second year to get a degree in accounting because that was the promise I made. My younger brother, Maximo graduated high school a couple months ago, but didn't have any plans to attend college. Big Jim had him slanging dope at fourteen and there wasn't shit me or Mauricio could do to get him away from the fast money.

I had my suspicions about Big Jim. Papí was getting money hand over fist. I knew there was money from their life insurance policy, as well as the money from the sales of our home, cars, and everything else. But my brothers and I had to work our asses off in the streets to have money in our pockets.

Big Jim got knocked for a murder charge a year ago but he was still running shit from behind bars. He had his right-hand Floyd handling shit on the street and we worked under him. I wasn't feeling that because the shit should've gone to Ricio. All of the drugs and the territory was started by papí. Without him, Big Jim wouldn't have nothing.

I went back in the trap after Ricio left and waited for the crew to come through to clean up the mess he'd made. I told everybody else to move around until shit was straight. Looking at the bodies that laid on the floor lifelessly, I had to walk away. There was a knock on the back door at the same moment my cell pinged with a text. Snatching it from my hip, I looked at the message and it was from Polo. He was the head of the cleanup crew. Opening the door, I stepped aside to let them in.

"What up, Sosa. What are we looking at?" he asked walking down the hallway.

"That damn Mauricio blasted two muthafuckas, sending them to meet their maker."

As we entered the room where the bodies were, Polo whistled loudly. "Damn, Ricio! What the fuck did baby girl do to that nigga? He is lucky I'm good at cleaning up messes like this. That nigga needs to calm his ass down before he has more enemies than he wants to have. It doesn't matter that he pays well, he is like a brother to me and I would hate for someone to come for him."

"I had a talk with him before he left and I hoped he took what I said to heart. All will be good, fam. Since you are here, I was gon' hit you up tonight anyway. Ricio's birthday is tomorrow and I have a surprise party planned on Friday night. We will be at Paradise Kitty's on Ontario, won't you come through and show the nigga some love. It will be an all-white party."

"Hell yeah, I'll be there. You know I couldn't miss out on celebrating my nigga's day. Text me all the details." He said as he and his workers started cleaning.

I wasn't about to watch them scoop up brain matter, so I went to the kitchen and sat down at the table. Talking about Mauricio's party with Polo reminded me that I needed to call Nija. She was the one I needed to get that nigga to the club.

Scrolling through my contacts, I pressed on her name and listened to the phone ring in my ear. I was about to hang up because I thought she wasn't going to answer, but she picked it up before it went to voicemail. I was glad she did because I wasn't leaving a message.

"Hey, Sosa. No, I haven't seen Ricio." She said into the phone.

"I'm not looking for him, I need to ask a favor. You know his birthday is tomorrow. I'm throwing him a party at Paradise Kitty on Friday. I need you to get him to the club for me. You are the only one I know that can get him there without raising suspicion."

She was quiet for a few seconds before she spoke. "Oh, that's great, Sosa. This party will lift his spirits since they are always low on his birthday. I will figure out a way to get him there, keep me posted. Is there anything else?"

"Nah, that's all I need. Thank you so much Nija, you always come through for his crazy ass. Too bad he don't realize he has a gem in you."

Nija hung up without responding to what I'd said. I tossed my phone on the table because I shouldn't have said that shit to her. I knew she loved his ass and he loved her too, but he couldn't leave the other hoes alone. Nija wasn't the type to play second fiddle to any nigga, that's what I liked about her. She stood up to his ass when he was wrong.

My phone buzzed on the table. Picking it up, I pressed the button to bring the screen to life and I had a text message. When I opened it, the biggest smile appeared on my face, it was a bitch named Jessica. She reached out at the right time, I needed the gushy that rested between her thighs to get my mind off the craziness of today.

Jessie: Are you coming to see me tonight?

Me: Yeah, I'm handling business right now, but I'll hit you when I'm on my way.

Jessie: Okay, I'll get her ready for you, baby.

I hated when she called me that shit, the only thing we did was fucked. There weren't any feelings involved this way, it stopped at me smashing, getting in those guts. I wasn't trying to be in a relationship with not one bitch. I was free to do whomever and whenever without anybody breathing down my back. I didn't even give them reason to believe it could go further.

"Polo, how much longer will y'all be? I got some shit I need to dive into."

"Give me about thirty minutes and we will be out of your hair."

They made good time because I was on the road to Jessica's crib forty minutes later. Speeding along the Dan Ryan expressway pushing the petal to the metal doing damn near a hundred miles an hour. Pussy would have a nigga breaking all kinds of laws to get to it, if that shit was good.

***

Pulling up on Jessica's block there were niggas out everywhere. That was the only thing I hated about coming to her spot. It was like time stood still when I stepped out of my midnight black Mercedes Coupe. I always dressed to the nines, it didn't matter what day of the week it was. Seeing me looking like a throwaway was never going to happen.

That day I had on a pair of white Balmain jeans, with a white Balmain tee that hugged my chest with my tats on display for all to see. I had on a pair of white Burberry 'Perforated checked' sneakers, yeah, I was on my all white kick for the day. The way the hoes were drooling, I knew I was looking good as fuck.

Being a light skinned nigga that was five feet eight inches tall with a low fade, bitches flocked to me like bees to honey. I looked more like my ma and the Dominican bloodline was strong. With a healthy joint to match.

I walked slowly up the walkway to Jessica's house and rang the doorbell. Turning around with my back facing the door, I glanced around the block and all eyes were still on me. I hit the alarm button on my key fob as I heard the locks turning from the inside of the house.

The door opened and Jessie was standing in the doorway looking sexy as she wanted to be. My lip instantly went between my teeth as I looked at her. She stepped to the side and allowed me entrance to her home. Before she closed the door, one of the niggas hollered out to her.

"What up, Jessica, wit yo' fine ass?"

She closed the door after waving and I laughed. Niggas always tried to stunt like they were proving a point. Shid, I didn't give a fuck. His ass could come through as soon as I left that muthafucka, she wasn't mine. That was the reason I traveled with gold wrappers, I didn't know what went on when I wasn't around.

Jessie sashayed her ass over to the couch where I sat. The way her hips swayed from side to side in the short skirt she wore, had my dick growing rapidly. Sitting down on my lap, she tried to kiss me in my mouth and I turned my head quickly. She scrunched up her face like she didn't know why she couldn't put her lips on me.

"Don't act like you don't know the rules, Jessie. We ain't never shared a kiss and we will not start today. Stand up," I said pulling an extra-large Magnum out of my pocket.

Kicking off my shoes, I unbuckled my belt and unbuttoned my pants. I lifted up off the couch and eased my pants down along with my boxers, draping them neatly on the coffee table. I stroked my pipe to life and covered him with the condom.

"Come sit on this muthafucka, Jessie."

She didn't hesitate to comply with what I asked of her. Raising the skirt over her thighs to her waist, I could see her ass cheeks from the front. That was one of her key attributes that I loved and I couldn't get enough of it. She straddled my lap and lowered her cat slowly on my dick. The head was the only part that entered her tunnel and she was constricting her muscles tightly around it.

"Mmmmmm, shit." I mumbled lowly. This shit happened every time I fucked her ass, she always had to tease a mutha-fucka first. I didn't come over for this love making shit, I came to fuck. Grabbing her firmly by the waist, I slammed her down on my erection.

"Ooooouuuu, yes!" Jessie screamed out as she rotated her hips. With every grind she had my toes curling. Her pussy was good and it seemed like it got tighter every time I came over. I didn't know what the fuck she did to keep that muthafucka in tip top shape, but she needed to keep it up.

I lowered my hand to her ass and inserted my middle finger deep inside. That's what she wanted, because she started bucking hard on my finger. I removed my finger and cupped her ass in my hands and stood up. Changing the position, I lowered her onto the couch with her knees resting on the cushions. She tooted her ass in the air because she knew what was about to happen.

"Open that ass up for me." I said standing back a little while she got herself ready for me.

Dropping to my knees with my joint in my hand, she reached back and spread her cheeks wide. I spit on her asshole and watched it cascade down the crack of her ass. Taking my thumb, I rubbed up and down until her ass was lubed up just right. I guided my dick to her dookie chute and inserted it slowly.

"Yes, Papi! You know how I like it. Fuck this ass the way I like it," she purred.

I got lost between her cheeks and started moving in and out faster. Her ass was contracting and making a popping sound that had my dick bricked up. Jessie was the only bitch I fucked that liked to get it in the ass and I loved that shit. She was throwing it back on me like she was running a marathon.

"Damn I love the way your ass grips my dick. You ready to take all this shit, girl?"

"Yessss, give it all to me." she moaned reaching back to cupping my balls.

The way I was slamming in her back doe, any other bitch would've been hollering stop. Jessie wanted me to keep going. That's why she was my star player. There was no limit to the things I could do to her. Feeling my nut tingling the very balls that she was gripping, I sped up my pace. My left hand went between her legs and I rubbed her bud fast and hard while I continued to open up her ass.

"I'm about to cum, Sosa!" she screamed out.

I continued to rub her clit and I felt it getting hard on my fingers. That was the cue to let me know she was about to make it rain in that muthafucka. I kept pounding my dick in and out of Jessie and her moans became louder. She started cursing my ass out because she was trying her best to hold that shit in.

"Yes, you nasty muthafucka! Fuck my ass harder, I'm about to cum!"

"Stop talking about the shit and let it go, Jessie. Uhhhhh, Uhhhhh, sssssss, shit!" I said trying to hold off on shooting my nut before she got hers.

I may have been a hard core nigga, but I made sure I left my mark on a bitch. I aimed to please and being selfish was not my forte. Stroking her clit faster, I felt the splash between her legs and the squeal followed behind it.

"Oooooouuuuu! Yessss! Aaaaaaah!" Jessie moaned while throwing her ass into my pelvis.

"Grrrrrrr, aaahhhhh, fuckkkkkk!"

I came so hard that my vision blurred and I got light-headed. Her ass was better than any pussy I had the liberty of fucking. That is the reason she would forever stay on my roster. Making sure I released all of my babies, I gathered my strength and eased my dick out. She plopped on the couch face first and I backed up. Leaving her laying there, I made my way to the bathroom to take a quick shower.

Flushing the condom down the toilet, I turned the water on in the shower before lifting the toilet seat to piss. Sleep was trying to make an appearance but I had shit to do. Plus, the only thing I did at a bitch house was fuck. There was never a time that I laid my head down and slept, unless it was at my own crib.

After stepping into the shower, the hot water cascaded down my body. I snatched up the bar of soap lathering every inch of me before stepping back under the spray of water. I placed my hand on the shower wall closing my eyes.

The images of my mom laid in the open casket appeared. Tears escaped my eyes easily. The last day I saw my mom was displayed vividly before my eyes. My blood started boiling and I instantly got mad. Every time a flashback appeared, someone ended up dying. Sometimes I could control it, other times I couldn't.

I jumped out of the shower and grabbed a towel out of the linen closet and dried off. Leaving the shower running for Jessica, I wrapped the towel around my waist. As I walked down the hall, I could see Jessie sifting through my pockets with her back turned.

The water was still running in the shower so, she assumed I was still in the bathroom. One thing I hated was a thieving bitch. If she needed something, all she had to do was ask a nigga and she would receive. With the way her ass felt, her stupid ass could get whatever the fuck she wanted from me. But she opted to take it.

Standing in the cut watching her ass, I wanted to see what she was going to do. She peeled off exactly seven hundred dollars because all I had on me were hundred-dollar bills. She put the money in her bra and put the rest back in my left front pocket. I pushed off the wall and started whistling as I walked into the room. She tried to sit back on the couch like she wasn't just going through a nigga's pocket. I laughed to myself because if I was a gullible nigga, I would've got ganked.

"What you doing, ma?" I asked calmly.

"I—nothing, just waiting on you. Are you about to head out, or are you gonna stay this time?" she asked sadly.

I held my head down because I couldn't believe this bitch was trying to play the 'being sad to see me go' role. "Jessie, you know I respect you like no other right?" She shook her head up and down. "You know if you need anything you can ask me for it, right?" shaking her head yeah again, I stormed toward her and grabbed her by her shirt. Reaching into her bra, I pulled out my money and slapped her ass with it.

Slap!

The bills went tumbling to the floor and her head whipped to the side. She chose to steal from me on the wrong day because the nigga that came out the bathroom, wasn't the same muthafucka that went in. I fucked up niggas but I didn't like when I had to beat the fuck out of a bitch. Jessie fucked up when she put her hand in the wrong cookie jar for a come up.

"If you know that all the fuck you had to do was ask, why the hell did you decide to steal from me?"

"I'm sorry, Sosa. I didn't think you would notice it was gone." She had the audacity to say.

Before I knew it, I'd punched her in the face a couple times. I hit her so hard blood flew out of her mouth. She tried to cover her face but my punches were too fast for her. I slapped the shit out of her and tossed her ass on the floor. Bending over to hit her ass I again, I stopped myself. I let the towel drop and put on my clothes.

Buckling my pants, I glared at her with disgust written on my face. "Don't ever dial my phone again. If I see your thieving ass again you better run in the opposite direction. Bitch I'm finished fucking with you! You are lucky as hell that I have a conscience because I could've left yo' hoe ass in this bitch stankin' over seven bills." I gritted as I stepped over her and walked out the door.

MEESHA

Chapter 3
Nija

My family moved to Chicago nine years ago when my mom got a promotion at her job. It was hard for me because leaving my friends wasn't something I wanted to do, but I didn't have a choice in the matter. Things were already kind of messed up in our household when my father left us to be with another woman. He showed up one day with a beautiful baby girl that was six months old at the time, in his arms. Yes, he brought the baby with him to tell my mama he was leaving her.

He still did what he was supposed to do and helped take care of my sister and I, but the situation damn near broke my mama. That's one of the reasons she didn't hesitate to take the job offer that relocated us. When we pulled up to the house in the Evergreen Park neighborhood, I fell in love with it from the start. That didn't mean I was happy to be there though. There were a couple teenaged girls sitting on the porch across the street. They appeared to be the around the age of my sister Nihiyah who was fourteen at the time.

Once the girls came over introducing themselves, my sister had three friends in less than ten minutes and I was standing there looking stupid. We had a week before we would start school and I already knew it was going to be hell trying to adjust. I watch the movers maneuver the furniture off the truck for a little bit before I went into the house to claim my room.

The house was much bigger than the apartment we had back in Oklahoma City, and I was glad about that. Nihiyah and I shared a room back home and I needed my own space to do what I wanted without having my every move watched. Climbing the stairs, I glanced down the right side of the hall, there were two bedrooms with a bathroom not too far away. I turned to look to my left and there was a bedroom that stood alone at the end of the hall.

I knew that room was going to be my mama's because it was away from the other two. Walking to the first bedroom, I looked inside and I knew right away that I wasn't going to like it because the closet was too small. I went to the other room and when I saw the bathroom inside, I was sold. That meant that I didn't have to leave my room for anything except to eat. The closet space was a tad bit bigger than the other room, but I had my own bathroom.

Walking to the window, I looked out and saw Nihiyah and her group of newfound friends talking to some guys. They were having fun while I was waiting for the movers to bring my things to my room. I decided to go downstairs and tell my mama which room I wanted. Finding her in the kitchen I waited until she ended her call.

"Hey ma, I know which room I want. Come on so I can show you," I said happily as soon as she said, "I'll talk to you later girl."

"Nija, I know you chose the one with the bathroom inside of it. But I picked that one out for Nihiyah, she is the oldest you know."

"Ma, Nihiyah hasn't even been inside this house since we got here. I saw it first and I like it. Please let me have it," I whined.

She thought about what I said and was about to respond when the movers came in with my bed. "Where do you want this, ma'am?" he asked.

She looked at me and smiled, "go show them where to put the bed, and you better keep the room clean at all times."

I ran upstairs leading the movers to my new room. Nihiyah was mad because she got the room that was left but that's what she gets for staying outside until dinner time. I spent the week helping my mama get the house together while Nihiyah hung out with her new friends. Mama was constantly fussing at her because she was always outside and barely helped with anything. The girls she befriended seemed kind of shady to me, but that was something she was going to have to deal with.

The first day of school came and I didn't know anyone. It felt odd going to a different school than my sister but she was in high school. During lunch I sat by myself eating the food I'd packed the night before. A group of girls walked past and one of them snatched my Capri Sun juice and kept walking. I was one of those bad-tempered girls so I continued to eat without saying anything, I didn't need to get in trouble for fighting.

A boy walked up to the girl and snatched the juice from her hand and said something that had her looking really scared. He came to the table where I was sitting and returned my juice before taking a seat in front of me.

"Hey, you're new here, huh?" he asked.

I didn't know what to say because I had never talked to a boy before so I shook my head and kept eating. Guys were like friends to me, I was what most adults called a tomboy. I played sports, chilled at the park, and played video games with boys, I didn't have any plans of doing anything else with them.

"You are going to have to start standing up for yourself. Tasia and her friends are straight bullies and if u let them keep picking on you, you are going to have a rough time at this school. I'm Mauricio, what's your name?" he asked.

"My name is Nija, and I don't care about them girls. If I wanted to, I could've gotten my own juice back. Fighting is something that I don't want to do, I've been in too much trouble behind it in the past. Best believe, I can hold my own. I just let the little shit slide today."

"If anybody messes with you, come tell me. I don't care who it is. You are new to the school so these girls are gon' try you, don't let them do it," he said.

From that day, he and I had been best friends. My feelings for him go beyond friendship though. We have done many things that couples did, but we haven't put a label on what we have. Mauricio was my homie, lover, friend that loved any kind of woman. I tried to stay away from him on that level but he was like a gnat that lingered around.

Whenever I even thought about being with a man, he found a way to cockblock like he was my man. I was always cussing him out about his actions because I never tried to shit on what he had going on. There were plenty of times I could've acted a whole ass, but I didn't.

Sosa called me and the first thing that came to mind was, he's looking for Ricio. I didn't have a clue where he was because I hadn't seen him in a couple days. Sosa explained that he was throwing Mauricio a surprised twenty-first birthday party at Paradise Kitty's strip club and he wanted me to get his brother there. I agreed but I didn't have a clue as to how I would pull it off.

I was sitting on the side of my bed from a long day of work and my stomach sent a reminder that I hadn't eaten. Being a caseworker at the Department of Human Services was so stressful. The job itself was easy, it's the people who are being serviced that made it unbearable at times. It wasn't my fault when someone didn't recertify on time or their benefits were cut for whatever reason, I was always the blame. I did my best to make the situation right but when you are screamed at, cussed out, and being called everything but a child of God, you tend to say fuck it. Sometimes I had to mentally remind myself that it was my job because I was ready to slap the shit out of some of the people that came to my desk.

Cooking was something I didn't feel like doing, so I picked my phone up to order takeout. As I thought about what I wanted, my phone started ringing. Looking down at the screen, Mauricio's name was displayed. Sosa had talked his brother up.

"What's up Ricio?" I bellowed out as I put the call on speaker.

"Why you screaming in my muthafuckin' ear, Nija?" he shot back.

"I wasn't screaming, my voice is high pitched and you know this already. Anyway, what you want?" I asked rolling my eyes as I slipped out of the slacks I had on.

"I was calling to tell yo' mean ass I was on my way to take you out to eat. Knowing you like I do, I bet you ain't ate all damn day."

"Don't act like you know me, Ricio."

"Tell me I'm wrong then, Ni."

I couldn't say anything because he was right. He always came through for me without me having to call. That was one of the things I admired about him. Mauricio was hard on the outside but could be really softhearted and loving at times. Many people said that he was a complete asshole because they didn't see the man as a whole. He only showed them what he wanted them to see.

"Just like I thought. Hurry up and get in the shower, by the time I get there you should be ready. You don't have to get all dolled up and shit, we aren't going anywhere spectacular this time around. I want to kick it with my favorite girl and have some fun. Is that all right with you?"

"Yeah, that's cool. I'll be ready." I said smiling from ear to ear. "See you when you get here."

"Bet," he said ending the call.

I rushed to the closet and decided to wear a pair of black capris', a hunter green halter top, with my green low top chucks. Laying the outfit out on the bed, I walked to the dresser and grabbed my black laced bra with the matching boy shorts. As I passed the mirror, I made a mental note to flat iron my hair and went into the bathroom.

I was moving fast as hell to get myself together. Drying off after my shower, I wrapped the towel around my body and plugged in the flat iron. Quickly brushing my teeth, I ran the flatiron through my hair, making sure my shit was laid. I did my makeup and went back into the room to throw on my clothes.

As I was tying my shoes, the doorbell rang. I grabbed my purse and stuffed my keys and phone inside as I made my way to the door. When I reached for the knob, this fool started ringing the bell repeatedly and my arm automatically dropped to my side. I hated when his ass got impatient. It irked my soul and the bad thing about it, he knew how I felt when he did it.

He started knocking on the door like he was the police and I snatched it open with force. "What I tell you about doing that? Damn you get on my nerves with your irritating ass."

Giving my body the once over, he shook his head. "Didn't I tell you not to get all dolled up, Ni?"

"I'm not dolled up, I grabbed something out of the closet and put it on. It's not my fault I look good in anything I put on," I said rolling my eyes.

"You are dolled up. The makeup, your hair straight as hell, and you smell good as fuck."

"Boy bye! This is me all day, every day, this ain't nothing new. You said that shit like I walk around looking like one of those bum bitches you seem to fuck with nowadays."

"That look don't look good on you, ma," he said laughing.

"What look would that be, Ricio?"

"Salty, mufucka! Outta all people, yo' ass should know that I don't remember what the fuck these hoes be having on. As long as my dick is satisfied, I don't give a fuck!"

"Well you need to care. Fuck around and let one of them wrap their lips around ya shit and catch something you can't get away from. Move the fuck back so I can lock my damn door!" I said pushing him in the chest.

I was low-key mad at what he said because he had everything he needed in me and didn't see it. Sweating a nigga was not something I would ever do. As much love that I had for Mauricio, I was not going to force it upon him to love me back the way I wanted him to. But when he sees me happy with another, he's not going to be a happy camper.

"Damn, why you got to put ya hands on a nigga though? You always set yaself up for the truth that flows effortless out of my mouth. I'm a real mufucka and if you don't want to hear facts, stop reaching."

Locking the door, I left his ass standing there and walked down the steps to his car. I stood by the passenger side of his money green 2018 Mercedes CLA Coupe. He took his time coming to the car and he still didn't pop the locks so I could get in. I shot him the meanest mug and he started laughing as he unlocked the doors.

I got inside and automatically fastened my seatbelt. As he got in the car, my phone chimed indicating I had a text message. My cheeks damn near touched my eyes as I read the message. Preparing myself to respond, my phone was snatched from my hand.

"Who the fuck got you smiling like you won the mufuckin' lottery or some shit?" He asked looking down at the phone. "Are you available to hang out tonight, beautiful?" he read the text out loud.

The only thing I could do was smirk at his ass because he was doing too much. Trying to get the phone back wasn't worth the effort because he would fuck around and throw it out the window. The text was from a guy I met one day on my lunch break. I was sitting alone and he asked if he could join me and I said sure. We enjoyed lunch, exchanged numbers, and kept in touch. Honestly this was the first time he ever asked to hang out at night.

Focusing my attention back on Mauricio, I noticed he was replying to the text on *my* phone. I tried to snatch it from his hand but he slapped my arm away. "Ricio, give me my phone! You don't have a right to reply to any texts that are meant for me." I attempted to get my phone back and failed a second time.

He looked at me as if he wanted to kill me, "I don't have a right? Get the fuck outta here with that bullshit, Ni. I paid the bill on this mufucka a year in advance! I can check this bitch for the next six months whenever I want to! Fuck you mean?" he gritted.

"It's not because I can't pay the bill myself, you went to the Sprint store and did that shit on your own. I didn't find out about it until I went to pay it and didn't have a balance! Give me my phone!"

Hitting the send button, he handed the phone to me. I looked down at the screen and gasped. This muthafucka was something else, I knew I wouldn't have to worry about the guy hitting my line again. Surely, he would put me on the block list immediately after reading Mauricio's reply.

"Really, Ricio?"

"What? I didn't do shit but tell that nigga what the fuck it is."

"Look fam, Nija don't need another nigga hitting her line but me. I got her in every way imaginable. You was just something to keep her occupied until I got back. Don't hit this line if you like breathing. Oh, and that wasn't a threat." I read out loud. "Do I take your phone and reply to them busted ass bitches you fuck with? You are always throwing a monkey wrench in shit when someone is trying to get to know me. I'm gonna need you to stop threatening people too! If you want to run niggas away, claim me as your own and then you would have the right to be mad. Until then, stay the fuck out of my personal business."

"That was cute," he said starting the car and backing out of the driveway. "You are my business, Nija. I don't have to claim you in order for you to know that you mean the world to me. I won't apologize for what I did because I'll do the shit again. But, I didn't come to scoop you up to argue the whole night. Let's enjoy our time together and make it count."

I didn't say shit to what he said because it was bullshit to me. We were cruising down the street for a few when he made a right onto 79th street. I was avoiding eye contact with Mauricio because he had truly pissed me off.

"What the fuck is this lil nigga doing now?" he said out of the blue as he whipped his car along the curb.

He jumped out of the car and stormed toward the liquor store on the corner. I let the window down because I couldn't really see what was going on. When I spotted Maximo, I knew all hell was about to break lose.

Mauricio and Sosa were trying to get him to stay off the streets but it wasn't working. He had just graduated from high school and he was determined to graduate from the University of Narcotics. Big Jim created a monster when he gave him his first pack to get off as a test, now he thought he was Nino Brown of Chicago and didn't know shit.

Maximo was beating the shit out of a dude on the side of the building. Mauricio ran up to him and yanked him off the guy. I could tell Mauricio was hollering at him but I couldn't hear the exchange. Whatever Maximo said, didn't sit well with his older brother. Mauricio punched him in the jaw and Maximo pulled his gun. I turned off the car and pocketed the keys before I jumped out to stop what was about to go down.

Chapter 4
Mauricio

Nija was mad at me for replying to the nigga that was on her phone trying to shoot his shot. What the fuck did she think I was going to do, sit there while she was skinning and grinning because of another nigga? Nah, that would never happen. It was quiet in the car but I refused to turn on the radio. I loved to hear her breath when she was frustrated, the sound alone turned me on.

I had bitches from here to Cali but Nija was one that would forever have a place in my heart. She was there through all the bullshit I had to go through after my parents died and I would forever be in debt with her. I did all that I could to make her life comfortable. That was the reason I paid her bills even though she begged me not to.

We started out as friends but it turned into something else one night while we were chillin' in my dorm. Getting in her guts and taking her virginity was not in the plans, that shit just happened. I knew I wasn't going to be exclusive with her because I was running up in any bitch that would spread them cheeks for me.

The feelings that I tried hard to keep at bay for her only emerged when I saw another nigga trying to move in. I knew the shit was foul because she deserved to be with someone that would make her happy, but in my mind, Nija was mine. One day I will stop playing games and cuff her ass and she would be right by my side permanently.

We were rolling down the Nine when I just so happened to look over at the liquor store. My lil brother Maximo was stomping a nigga the fuck out. Without thinking, I curbed my ride and hopped out. I snatched his ass off the nigga by the back of his neck.

"What the fuck are you doing, Max? You love putting on a show for these niggas, don't you?" I was referring to the dumb mufuckas that were standing around cheering his goofy ass on while he broke dude up. "This is what they want you to do! This stupid shit could leave you behind bars. With the shit you out here doing, you might want to keep a low profile from the law, stupid mufucka! I bet yo' ass dirty as fuck too. This is the reason you need to take yo' ass to school!"

"Man fuck what you talking about, Ricio! That school shit was for you and Sosa, I ain't wit it. My calling is to slang these rocks out here. College can't teach me shit about the streets. I'm a grown ass man and you niggas can't tell me what the fuck to do with my life. It worked all those years that I didn't have a choice, but it won't work no mo. So, you can get the fuck outta my face trying to be a big brother because I don't need yo' ass. I'm good with holding Big Jim down until he gets back out in these streets."

Before I could stop myself, I hauled off and rocked his ass. His head whipped to the side and he spit out the blood that filled his mouth. I was mad at the way he had outright disrespected me but I wasn't expecting what the lil nigga did next. Swinging back around to face me, I was face to face with a .38 chrome.

Chuckling like a hyena, I couldn't believe this mufucka was treating me like an op. "Brother or not, I hope you know what the fuck to do with that mufucka. Make yo' one shot count because if you don't, my mama is gon' have to forgive me because you gon' die behind this shit. You want to act tough, I'm gon' give you the chance to show these pussy mufuckas what yo ass about."

His hand was shaking because my little brother wasn't about that life. He didn't train stupidly like Sosa and I did and I knew he wasn't a match for me. I was taught that a scared man, was a deadly man. All it would take was for him to get too scared and squeeze the trigger slightly.

"Y'all are not about to do this! Max, put the gun down, now! This is your brother!" Nija screamed as she got between the two of us.

"Nija, go back to the car!" I screamed keeping my eyes on Maximo's hand that held the gun.

"I'm not going anywhere! Y'all family and this wouldn't be right if your fa—"

"You can stop right there because my papí would be fuckin' him up right now for the choices that he has made, better yet for the shit that was forced upon him! Big Jim ain't about his ass, but he's idolizing that nigga!"

"He was the only person that looked out for me when papí got gunned down!"

"Max, put the gun away, please. Y'all can talk about this like brothers, without weapons."

I had to scratch my head on that shit because if it wasn't for me and Sosa, his ass would've been out there doing something strange for the lil change Big Jim had him working his ass off for. He lowered the gun and I wanted to punch his ass again but with Nija standing between us, it wasn't going to be possible without hitting her in the process.

"Big Jim wasn't the only one to do shit for yo' punk ass! You ain't nothing but a check to him. I was the one that tried to bring you up the way papí wanted me to! You let this dope shit go to ya head and now you're down for the cause, nigga you still got a lot to learn. But I'm gon' let your hardheaded ass do you out in these streets. Don't call me for shit because I won't be there to bail your mark ass out! Call Big Jim and let me know how that works out for you!" I said walking back to my car.

"Fuck you, Ricio! I don't need you, nigga!"

Those eight words paralyzed me for a minute and I went charging at his ass full force. Once again, Nija stepped in front of me preventing me from reaching out to touch that bastard. "Fuck me? Nah, fuck *you,* homie. "Tan pronto como sepa lo que necesito saber, Big Jim está cayendo. Espero que no estés en la línea de fuego cuando todo golpea al ventilador. Me estoy moviendo de cualquier manera que se interponga en mi camino, incluyéndote a ti si es necesario, hermano." (As soon as I find out what I need to know, Big Jim is going down. I hope you not in the line of fire when everything hits the fan. I'm moving any and everything that gets in my way, including you if it comes to that, brother.)

"I'll be ready, make sure you are." He said with a smirk on his face.

Nija stayed back to talk some sense into his dumb ass, I was done with him. Everything my papí said about taking care of my brothers went out the window when he upped that thang on me. Him being my brother was the only reason he was able to get away with that shit. If it was any other nigga, they would be hosing his brains off the sidewalk.

The door opened and Nija climbed inside of my ride. The hurt was visible on her face. She loved my brothers like they were her own, she had never seen me and Max go at it like that. But it wouldn't be the last time as long as Big Jim was in his ear. I knew what I had to do though, I had to go holla at Beast before I had to kill Max's ass.

Snatching my keys from her hand, I put the car in drive. We were headed to the Italian restaurant that she loved so I could feed her. To be honest, I didn't even want to sit down and eat anymore. While I was waiting for the light to change, I pulled my phone out and ordered our food through the app and decided to go in to pay for it. The shit with Maximo had me in a different mood all together.

"Do you mind that I ordered our food to go? We can crash at my crib for the night." I glanced at her quickly then pressed the gas.

"That's fine, but I have to go to work in the morning, Ricio. I'm going to need to go home tonight."

"You know damn well you have clothes at my crib, don't try that shit, Ni. If you would rather go home, I don't have a problem taking you back. I figured with my birthday being tomorrow, there's no one else I'd rather bring it in with than you."

She was quiet for a moment and I looked over at her to see her reaction. Her face didn't show any emotion so I kept driving. I pulled in front of the restaurant and hopped out to grab the food. It didn't take long before I was back out in the car. I sat for a minute looking at her after putting the food on the back seat. "What's it gon' be?"

"We can go to your house, Ricio," she said lowly.

The commute to my crib seemed like it was taking forever. I hit the button to turn the radio on and Musiq Soulchild's "Teach Me" blared through the speakers. I didn't know if that was a sign from above for me to do right by Nija or not. My mind wasn't in a place to love her like I wanted to at that moment.

Vibing to the lyrics, there was no doubt Nija was that special someone who could teach me to love. Turning twenty-one was only hours away, and there was plenty of pussy out there for me to play around with that didn't mean shit. I was still a young nigga and I wanted to make sure I was ready to settle down before I went after Nija on some serious shit.

I hit the button for the underground garage door to open and made my way to my designated parking space. Nija was the only woman that was allowed to step foot in my crib. I took all them other hoes to the telly or one of the trap houses.

I was taught not to bring shit that didn't mean nothing to me to my spot.

Opening the door, I went around to her side of the car and opened the door for her. When she was out, I got the food out the back and locked up. Nija was already at the elevator waiting and it opened as soon as I stepped up. I lived in a two-bedroom condo downtown. The only people that knew where I laid my head were family, Big Jim didn't even know.

We walked down the hall and Nija had her keys out already entering my spot. I trusted her enough to have a key and she knew more than enough just in case something happened to me. She was my Bonnie and I was her Clyde, we had that type of connection. As I stepped inside, she closed and locked the door before removing her shoes. I kicked off my J's and went straight to the kitchen.

My phone rang and I snatched it off my hip, it was Sosa. "What up?"

"What the fuck happened on the Nine? Max called and said you almost got shot over there, do we have a problem with them niggas?" I started laughing heartily and doubled over because my stomach cramped up. "I'm lost, fam. What's so funny?"

"Did yo' lil brother tell you that his punk ass was on the other end of the barrel? I didn't think so. I'm done with his ass Sosa, he is solely your responsibility. When he pulled his piece on me, I could've—"

"Hol' up, run that shit by me again."

"You heard me right, brah. I saw his ass on the Nine beating the shit out of this young dude while his boys cheered his stupid ass on. He got mad disrespectful and I rocked his ass! Lil brother or not, disrespect is disrespect. The mufucka pulled his tool and told me that he didn't need me as long as he had Big Jim. That nigga said fuck me! Fuck me, out of all people, he chose another mufucka over me! Yeah, I'm done with his ass. If it wasn't for Ni, I would have forced him to shoot his mufuckin' self."

Talking to Sosa only infuriated me all over again. Nija entered the kitchen and started unpacking the food. She set everything on the table and grabbed plates for the two of us. I was watching her every move, she always fit right in when she was in my home with me. I didn't have to tell her where anything was, she already knew. This was just as much her home as it was mine, she opted to come over every so often as of late. My brother cut into my thoughts when his voice boomed through the earpiece.

"Max didn't say none of that shit to me, bro!"

"Of course, he didn't with his pussy ass! If he gets into anything my phone bet not ring with his ass on the other end. I won't be there to help his ass out, I put that on my mama."

"Ricio, you can say that shit all day, if he gets into anything you and me both will be there."

"Sosa, I'm done with Maximo Vasquez, dog. He wants to be that nigga in the streets, he can learn that shit on his own. I'm done. As a matter of fact, I'm calling Beast so he can talk to him before I kill him."

"I'm gon' call him when I get off the line with you because he had me thinking I had to gear up to add to my body count. He didn't tell me he was the muthafucka that was holding steel on ya. Actually, I'm about to see where he at and he is about to get fucked up tonight. He will be calling to apologize, so be on the lookout for his call."

"Don't send that boy off, man. He bet not call my shit. I don't want his mufuckin' apology. Max can kiss my ass! He's all yours now, I'm through with him. But I'm about to hit up Beast so I can eat with my favorite lady."

"You need to stop playing with that girl before you lose her ass, Ricio. Nija is the girl for you. I've been telling you that shit for years, brah."

"What makes you think it's Nija that I'm referring to?"

"Please, nigga. There isn't another bitch that you refer to as your favorite girl other than mama. Handle your business and Happy birthday, nigga. I may not talk to you when the clock strikes twelve."

"Thanks, brah, I appreciate that shit. Until tomorrow man, love," I said disconnecting the call.

Nija was eating and reading something on her phone. She really hadn't said anything since the incident with Max. I didn't invite her over to give me the silent treatment, I could've pulled that shit off by myself.

"You want to tell me what's on your mind, Ni? I asked you over to keep me company so I wouldn't be alone for my birthday, ma."

"I'm here, Ricio. The shit between you and Max is fucked up. He was wrong for what he did and even for what he said, but I don't think you should turn your back on him. With the shit that you speculate about Big Jim, do you think it's wise to leave him out there by himself with Big Jim's people?"

"He won't be alone, he got Sosa to back him up. I'm done fuckin' with him Ni, you heard the way he was talking. Them niggas been feeding my brother shit against us, it shows in the way he blatantly got that shit off his chest. Max is about to learn the hard way that nothing comes before family."

I sat down and tried my best to eat the lasagna that I'd ordered, but my appetite wasn't there. Getting up with my plate in hand, I placed it inside the microwave for later. Nija wasn't going to let it sit in there, she would cover it and place it in the refrigerator before she left the kitchen.

"I'll be on the balcony. I have to call Beast and fill him in on what transpired. Pick out a movie or something, we still have a couple hours before my birthday."

She nodded her head and continued to eat. Walking to my bedroom, I went into my emergency stash and rolled a fat blunt filled with purp. Smoking wasn't my thing but when I was stressed, it mellowed me out. When I was in the streets, there was no drinking and smoking going on. Only in the comfort of my home and I had to be in for the night. Making my way back to the living room, I opened the sliding glass door that led to the balcony. Sitting in the nearest chair I placed the call to Beast.

"What up, boi? It's not ya birthday yet, I was gon' call." he answered in his deep baritone.

"I know you would've called but I'm not trying to recite this shit on my day, so I decided to give you a call beforehand about Max. The lil nigga pulled a gun on me tonight."

"We got to be talking about another Max because I know damned well you're not talking about my nephew Max."

"That's exactly who I'm talking about. He had the nerve to disrespect me and follow it up with a slap in the face. According to him, Big Jim is the only person that has done anything for him. Max said fuck me and he didn't need me, so I rocked his ass. He grew balls when he pulled that pistol on the one nigga that has been watching his back, but that shit is dead after tonight. I don't know what the fuck Big Jim and his crew is putting in his head, but something ain't right with them mufuckas. I'm gon' find out what's going on because things been very fishy for the past four years. I just can't put it together."

"I can't believe Max, but I will definitely hit his ass up. I dare him to jump hard with me, I'll walk to cave his muthafuckin' chest in. Enough about that shit, there's other things that we must discuss, but it won't be done tonight over the

47

phone. In approximately two hours, you will be twenty-one. As well as the King Pin of Chicago."

"Wait what?" I was confused as hell by what he said, I didn't understand.

"Come to my crib early tomorrow and I will fill you in. It's time to put your father's plan into motion." Beast said and hung up.

The words he said echoed in my head but I didn't understand what they meant. I ran a trap for Big Jim but I was nowhere near ready to run drugs through a whole city while I distributed that shit to my own workers. Shaking the conversation from my head, I took a couple pulls from my blunt and went inside. Nija had finished eating and was sitting in the living room waiting for me with *Love & Basketball* paused on the tv. Every time I let her choose the movie, that was the one she always picked. I didn't complain, I just went and sat on the couch and allowed her to lay between my legs to enjoy her favorite movie.

Chapter 5
Beast

Sitting in my lounge chair watching the highlights from the Notre Dame football game, my phone started vibrating in the cup holder. When I looked down to see who was calling, it was Mauricio. I had planned to call him at the stroke of midnight to wish him a happy birthday, but he beat me to the punch.

As I listened to him recite what Max did and the words that he threw at him, I knew it was time to tell him the truth. Being quiet until the moment presented itself was hard, but I had to do things in the way I was instructed.

Maurice "Reese" Williams was my best friend from diapers until his untimely death. Our mothers were best friends as well. They conceived months apart. Reese and I were raised as brothers and the bond never wavered. We got into so much shit together back in the day, but never turned on one another.

We both went off to college at Northeastern Illinois University where I played football and Reese just played in pussy. When we graduated, I joined the Army and felt bad because I left him all alone. Staying in contact was a must because that's the way we were raised. After four years of serving my country, my enlightenment was over. At the time, I made up my mind that I wasn't reenlisting for the bullshit that was waiting in Afghanistan.

Going back to Chicago was a must for me because that's where my family was. I didn't know what I was going to do with my life. Reese was a manager at Foot Locker and he voiced how much he hated it daily. I decided to try out for Pro football after a while because it had always been my passion. Plus, I had plans to make millions and I was going for it.

I tried out for the Pittsburg Steelers twice, Carolina Panthers, as well as the Charlotte Rage Arena football team before my knees gave out, and I was done. Filing for my VA disability was tough because I had to go back and forth with them for my shit. Fighting hard, I didn't give up. Eventually, I walked away with a quarter mil and that's when me and Reese's life changed for the better.

When I was in the Army, I met a dude named Felipe while stationed in El Paso, Texas. He was always telling me stories about how his uncle Jorge was a Columbian drug lord. I wasn't into that type of shit but I listened all the same, not knowing the relationship I built would set me straight.

One night, Felipe and I went out to have a good time on our off day. A group of Mexicans approached him on some bitch shit. They knew not to approach me because I was a muthafucka that stood six foot four, weighing in at two hundred eighty-two pounds of pure muscle that could silently fuck shit up. Trained in Taekwondo and Silat, I didn't need a gun to end a life, my body was a deadly weapon.

Felipe on the other hand was a scrawny dude. He had heart and could hold his own, but he was no match for the four assailants that surrounded him. I stood up and one of the guys reached for something on his hip while another guy punched Felipe in the face, it was on from there.

I automatically went for the guy with the weapon so he wouldn't be able to use what he had in his hand on Felipe. Wrapping my arm around his, I constricted on it to force him to drop the knife he was clutching in his fist. Using my other hand to hold down his left arm, I kicked him in his groin. When he doubled over, I grabbed him by his neck and squeezed until he passed out.

Dropping him to the ground, I was hit from behind. That only enraged me more because I was snaked. When I swung my body around, the guy had pulled an icepick from his pocket. These muthafuckas needed weapons but I was willing to show them that they rolled up on the wrong nigga. He charged at me quickly swinging the pick. Blocking his attack at his forearm, I hit his shoulder and swept his feet from under him. As he lost his balance, I grabbed him by the head and snapped his neck. I didn't have time to play with these muthafuckas. Being in the Army put me in the mindset of, kill or be killed and I wasn't ready to die.

Felipe was beating the hell out of the guy that punched him and the fourth guy was nowhere in sight. I watched him beat the dude to a pulp. The guy's face was unrecognizable and he was wheezing through his nasal cavity. Felipe sent a blow to his chest and the crack of the bone was heard vividly. He was dead before he hit the ground.

We survived that night and the police never found out who killed those guys. Neither one of us were worried. I received a call on my cell a couple days later and it was Jorge. He thanked me for being there for his nephew and guaranteed he'd be there if I ever needed anything. When that settlement came through, I knew I wanted to flip a nice chunk of that shit.

I hit Jorge up and the rest was history. He tried to hit me with my first ten bricks for free, but that's not how things worked in this game. I was always taught, ain't shit free in the streets. I paid for the work and we distributed that shit like hotcakes at Ihop. We had the city of Chicago on lock in a matter of a couple of years. Being a drug dealer was never in my plans, I was more of a behind the scenes muthafucka. I handed everything to Reese but I was still standing ten toes down with him while getting money.

Waking up going straight to the kitchen to start the coffee maker, my day wasn't right without it. As the aroma filled the air, I closed my eyes and my body started tweaking with anticipation of the caffeine that it was craving. A pair of hands wrapped around my waist bringing me back to the present.

"Good morning, baby."

I turned around and looked down in the face of my flavor of the day. Sincere was one of the bitches that I entertained from time to time. At forty, I still wasn't ready to be in a relationship. If I decided to settle down, Sincere would be the one I kept around. Her skin reminded me of a cup of mocha flavored coffee. She had a body that would throw you off your game. Titties sat high and perky, thirty-eight double Ds stayed staring a nigga in the face, slim waist, and an ass that you could see from the front with a camel toe that stood out in everything she covered it with.

"Good morning. I have a meeting with my nephew so I'm gon' need you to shake. I have to discuss some important shit with him, but I will hit you up as soon as we're finished. I'm gon' need another dose of that power pussy you possess," I said kissing her lips while I grabbed a handful of her ass.

"I understand, business before pleasure. You know when you send the dick signal, I'll be here faster than a superhero. I'm going to give you a pass for last night because I see you had something huge on your mind, don't do anything crazy, Erique."

"Don't act like you know me, Sin. Things will be all good, believe that. I can't promise things won't get crazy. The mind-set that I'm in is Beast mode, Erique is playing in the background. I don't want you to worry your little head about me, I ain't going nowhere, that's something I can promise. Now, go upstairs and get dressed, Ricio should be here any minute," I said letting her go to pour a hefty cup of java.

"Erique—Beast, it's been years since I've seen you in this frame of mind. Back then it wasn't a good thing, the streets are not what they used to be. The niggas out there are ruthless, they don't give a fuck about anything or anyone."

"And I do?" I asked looking over my shoulder with a grimace on my face. "I don't give a damn about any nigga out in the streets. They bleed just like me. I won't get dirty unless I have to. If I have to put in work, the streets will hear my roar and get the fuck outta my way. Until then, let me handle my business."

I leaned against the counter as I sipped from my favorite Notre Dame mug. Sincere had been around since I came home from the Army. She had seen the good, the bad, and the ugly. What I loved about her was the fact that she didn't mind getting her hands dirty and she was riding regardless. She always tried to talk me out of a lot of shit, but didn't hesitate to turn into Sin City when the time came. She was nothing nice when she was in that element. Beauty, brains, and deadly as hell. Shit made my dick rock up every time I thought about it, that's why she was my bitch.

"Okay, let me get out of your hair. I'll get up with Leslie and go shopping or something. Hit my line when you're ready for me," she said heading out of the kitchen. Abruptly spinning back around, "oh yeah, that bitch Sable called your phone while you were sleeping. I had to check her ass for calling herself coming at me disrespectfully. I will snatch her fucking tongue out through her throat. Talk to that hoe and let her know her place before she come up missing," she didn't wait for me to respond, she just turned and walked out of the kitchen and headed upstairs.

Chuckling as I grabbed my dick, I was about to go upstairs and get all up in her ass when the doorbell stopped me in my tracks. Her rant replayed in my head and I wanted to ignore the door all together, but I knew Mauricio was on the other side. I opted to let him in instead, that boss shit would be on my mind all day and I was going to ball her up soon enough.

"Happy birthday, lil nigga!" I said as I opened the door giving him a manly hug. Mauricio looked like his damn daddy so much, it brought tears to my eyes because I missed my nigga.

"Thanks man, twenty-one is about to have ya boy out here flossin'," he said laughing.

"As long as you do it the right way. Keep ya circle small and you will be alright. There are plenty of snakes out here in this cruel world. After today, things will be different for you, mark my words," I said stepping to the side so he could enter.

Leading the way to the living room, Sincere walked her sexy ass down the stairs looking like a whole five course meal at seven in the morning. She had on a pair of tight jeans that hugged her hips nicely. The off the shoulder blouse she wore did nothing to hide how big her titties were. She had on a pair of stilettoes that made her legs look endless and I was loving the sight before me. I was fighting the urge to take her back upstairs to my bedroom. Hearing Mauricio whistle loudly, I knew his ass was about to act up.

"Got damn, Sin! It's too early to be shitting on these hoes like that. Unc, you hitting that shit right, nigga!" he yelled pushing my shoulder.

"Respect my shit, youngin. Don't get beat the fuck up on your birthday, muthafucka. That's still my bitch, now calm that shit down." I said grilling his ass.

"My bad, I had to give her props because she out here killing shit. No disrespect, Sin, how you doing?"

"I'm good, Ricio. Long time no see and happy birthday. Hold on, I got something for you," she said walking into my office. Coming back out with a long box wrapped in gold wrapping paper, she handed it to him. "I had to give you

54

something special for your twenty-first birthday, I hope you like it," she said smiling.

Mauricio carefully tore the paper off exposing a black velvet jewelry box. He looked up with an inquiring stare and slowly opened the lid. He smiled big as he lifted a platinum linked chain out for us to see. He focused on the 'RB' charm that was filled with diamonds.

"This mufucka go hard! Thank you! Damn Sin, this is nice, what's with the RB?"

"I felt I should get you something that you could rock with your daddy close to your heart. The RB stands for 'Reese Boy'."

Ricio stood there quietly for a few seconds before he looked up with his eyes glistening with tears. Holding them at bay, he opened his arms for a hug. When she walked into his embrace, he held her tightly and cried like a baby. I knew he missed his father just as much as I did.

"I appreciate this so much, thanks again," he said kissing her cheek.

"No problem, enjoy your day. I'm gonna head out and let you guys talk," she said turning to stare at me. "I'll see you later big daddy," she said kissing my lips lightly.

I watched her ass switch all the way to the door and was still staring after she was gone. Thinking of all the ways I was going to wax all that when she came back was pure enjoyment, I couldn't wait to act on it. When I glanced at Mauricio he was laughing softly.

"What the fuck you laughing for?"

"Man Unc, stop playing and make an honest woman out of Sin. She has been around forever and you can tell she loves yo' ass. I don't know why, but she does."

"She ain't going nowhere, when I get to that point, she is the first in line. I'm not ready, one day though."

"I feel you on that. Having options is where it's at, you don't have to worry about none of these hoes questioning you about shit. I'm not loyal to nan bitch except my mama and she ain't here." His tone went down a couple of octaves when he spoke those words.

"With that being said, I guess it's time to talk, let's go into my office." I said grabbing my coffee, leading the way.

As I got comfortable behind my desk, he looked around at all the pictures I had hanging on the wall like it was his first time seeing them. I had every picture that I had of Reese on the walls. Majority of them were of the two of us together. The one he focused on the longest was the wedding picture that displayed his parents. I knew he was coming over so I removed the picture of my nigga laid out sharper than a knife in his casket. That's the one I'd spent hours on end staring at to prepare me for the moment I would have to tell Mauricio what was real and what was fake.

"I talked to Max last night, that muthafucka wants me to snatch a knot out of his ass. His mind has been poisoned, but when I see him, I'm fucking him up. I've been around all y'all lives and the disrespect that I got from him, is something that I won't accept. As he spit venom from his mouth, all I heard in my mind was 'fuck him up, Beast'. That's exactly what I plan to do too."

"That's what I was thinking when he pulled that tool on my ass. The only thing that saved him was Nija. He's my lil brother, but he crossed the line last night. I wanted to kill his ass, Unc. On the strength of family is the reason he was not scooped up and rolled into a meat wagon. I'm done. I hate to turn my back on him, but the nigga idolizing Big Jim over my Papí's legacy. That's a slap in the mufuckin' face like he is saying, fuck Reese Williams!"

Mauricio was hot for the shit Max did, I didn't blame him. I never got in the way of Reese's rants, I wouldn't get in Mauricio's way either. God cloned my best friend because I swear his son's mannerisms were the same as his. Now I had to see how strong his drive was, as well as how angry he could get. I needed him to turn into a monster when I reveal what I've waited years to tell him about.

"Sit down, Ricio. I have some shit that I need to lay on you. I want you to hear me out with an open mind." I sat with my hands folded in front of me, waiting to see if he had anything to say. When he didn't respond, I kept going as I reached inside the cabinet to retrieve a bottle of Remy VSOP and two glasses. "Your father and I had been in the drug game for a very long time. I stepped out of the limelight and let him handle shit on the streets. He formed a crew of niggas to help him move millions of dollars of product, monthly. He came to my house one day telling me that he felt something was going to happen to him, that happened a few weeks before he was killed. Big Jim and Floyd were the ones on his radar strongly. Hundreds of thousands of dollars were missing throughout the years. Big Jim was the one overseeing the money because he was quote en quote his closest friend next to me. Come to find out, he was robbing your father blind. Reese had no clue because he was getting money hand over fist and he didn't miss the money. Big Jim got greedy and tried his hand at stealing larger amounts. When Reese took it to him, he placed the blame on a young nigga that lost his life by the hands of your father and myself. At that point, I went over Reese's records and saw exactly when the shortage started. It took weeks to come up with the evidence but by the time I got it together, he was dead."

"How the fuck is this mufucka still breathing years after my daddy died!" Mauricio yelled jumping up. "You knew this shit and yo' ass sat back and did nothing! How the fuck is that possible, Beast? You better have a strong explanation for this shit because right about now, you ain't looking no better than his bitch ass!"

I couldn't do anything except let him get everything off his chest. He had every right to be furious over the things that I told him. My reaction would've been just as bad, so I didn't try to take that from him. What I did was told him why I waited, and why I didn't react.

"Have a seat, nephew. I —"

"Fuck that! I'm cool right here! Explain yo'self, Beast."

Running my hand down my face, I poured myself a hefty shot of Remy and downed it. I placed the glass on the desk and stared him in his eyes. "I want you to know that not saying anything was the hardest thing I've ever had to do. Why I didn't act was because, your father gave me strict instructions not to." I said opening the drawer on the top right side of my desk.

I gathered the stack of papers that I had placed in the drawer and put them in front of me. I had documentation after documentation of how Reese ran his organization. There was evidence on how much heroin, coke, meth, ecstasy, and percs that were sold monthly. His net worth was also amongst those documents. Along with written documentation that stated how to handle everything if he was to leave this earth. I also had a copy of the document Big Jim presented to the courts to gain custody of the kids.

"Mauricio, the answers to all of your questions sits right here," I explained slapping my hand on top of the paperwork. "Before I get into what's in the content of these papers, I want you to listen to something." I reached into the same drawer and pulled out a disk and inserted it into my Mac computer.

As we waited for the disc to load, Mauricio reached over grabbing the Remy bottle and poured a full glass. He threw the dark liquor back like a champ, going in for more. I didn't attempt to stop him until he downed a double shot and reached for the bottle a third time.

"That's enough, Ricio. I need you to be able to comprehend what I'm about to tell you. When everything comes to light, I don't want you to be too fucked up to remember." I said as I moved the bottle out of his reach.

"How the fuck did you expect me to react, Beast? You just told me some shit that you could've prevented, or at least handled! It seems to me, you didn't give a fuck about Papi!"

"I won't allow you to question the love I had for Reese! He was my nigga, my brother, before you were even a figment of his imagination, muthafucka! I stood down only because he told me he had Big Jim under control. I never stopped searching for the information he inquired about. The only thing I'm guilty of is not being there the night he was killed. The reason being, I had major surgery on my knee, but when you called, I got there as fast as I could. But that didn't matter because my boy was gone! I'm hurting over his death just as much as y'all, if not more. Don't ever discredit my loyalty to him." I glared.

Pinching the bridge of my nose, I took deep breaths before I reached out and touched his ass. The assumptions he spewed pissed me off but I knew I couldn't act the way I wanted. With everything he said, at the end of the day, he was still my family. I was going to stand by him and his brothers until I took my last breath on this earth. Grasping the mouse, I clicked the play button to start the disc I had inserted in the computer.

"All the shit you said—" His words were stuck in his throat when Reese's voice flowed through the speakers.

"My nigga! I hope all is well with yo' ass. It's game time, bro! Let's send these muthafuckas to the grave. The fact that you're listening to this disc, only means they got to me. I'm sorry for keeping you out of the loop about everything, but I'm a grown ass man that thought I had shit under control. Obviously, I didn't but that's water under the bridge. Listen to me and listen good, Beast. I put a lot of shit into play ahead of time because I knew they were gunning for me. The insurance policy has been updated, listing you as the primary beneficiary. Your name has been added to all of my business accounts too. The joint account that me and Maritza has is still in both of our names and that will stay the same for her and the boys to live off of. Money will transfer from the business account to that account every month, don't change the dollar amount until the day I stop breathing. Maritza gets the house and the cars. I want you to keep an eye on my wife, man. I think that nigga is up to something, I don't know what though."

"Pause that shit, unc!" I did what he asked and waited on him to speak. "Papí is running so much down in a recording that was done before he died. Are you sure you didn't have a clue about any of this?" Mauricio asked sitting up in the chair.

"I didn't know things were as deep as they were. If I had, we would've been on top of it together. Your father had me to help him out of so much shit all our lives, I'm guessing he wanted to do this on his own to prove that he didn't need anyone." I said lowly.

"Papí was concerned about mama's safety, he never said anything about that either?"

I hated the fact that he didn't fill me in on that concern because if he had, Maritza would be alive today. "No, he didn't." I answered truthfully.

"Since all this shit happened, there has been a question that never left my mind. I want you to answer this truthfully because I already know the answer but I need confirmation. Was my mama on drugs?"

The look in his eyes had a glimmer of hope in them. I knew for a fact that Maritza didn't do any drugs, she didn't drink anything stronger than coffee. "No, your mother didn't like what your father did to make money. She wanted him to stop a long time ago, she didn't smoke nor drink. The next question is going to be, how did she overdose, right?"

"Yeah, that's exactly where I was going with it. If she didn't do any hard drugs, how the hell did the needle end up in her arm? That was my thought process then, but now after hearing some of the things papí mentioned, this shit got Big Jim written all over it."

"Maritza's death definitely wasn't an overdose. I argued that fact to the detectives on the case but without proof, nothing could be done. I didn't receive the package that contained the disc and documents until a month after your mother's funeral. By that time, Big Jim had already presented the documentation to gain full custody of your brothers." I shuffled through the papers until I found the one I was looking for. Sliding the paper across the desk for him to look over.

"Why would papí sign us over to him and not you?"

"He didn't. Let's keep listening." I said as I pressed play and Reese's voice filled our ears once again.

"I found a falsified documentation at his house that would give him custody of Sosa and Max. I didn't think anything of it because it was useless without being notarized. Big Jim was smarter than I gave him credit for. Watch out for my wife, he's looking to take over my shit. Don't let it happen, I need you to step up as my brother. In a little over four years, retirement will be over for you, Beast. You will be the connect again. Once again, you're going to help flood the streets of Chicago with the purest cocaine from Columbia. On Mauricio's twenty-first birthday, you are to play this recording for him. There is a key to a safe deposit box at Citi Bank taped to the inside of the manila envelope the discs were in, as well as a key to a storage space that I own. Inside that locker is one hundred and fifty bricks that I vacuumed sealed tightly. The money received from the load belongs to y'all, I already paid Jorge for them. Big Jim is probably living the lavish life trying to be me. When it's time, I want Mauricio sitting on my throne as the Kingpin of Chicago."

The recording was silent for a few seconds before it cut off. Mauricio had tears rolling down his face and the veins protruded out of his temples, while his jaw constricted rapidly. I pushed another disc toward him that had his name on it.

"This is for you to listen to on your own. Right now, I must run down a couple things to you. Big Jim and Floyd didn't expect anyone to find out their connection to your father's murder—"

"And my mama's! Don't leave that shit out."

"That's correct. They didn't expect it to come to light and I've been waiting for this day to execute this plan. With the help of the Warden at the Prison, I've scheduled a visit for you to go to the prison to talk to Big Jim. Get everything off your chest but keep your voice down, and stay calm. Remember, you are going to a prison, keep ya attitude under control. Most importantly, let his ass know that you are coming for what's rightfully yours. Are you ready for this shit, Ricio?"

"Hell Yeah, I'm ready. Big Jim don't know what the fuck he did when he put me and Sosa in these streets. He prepared us for what papí had planned and had no clue. But they better get ready because—" he paused and snatched the box that Sin gave him earlier off the desk and opened it. Taking the chain out and putting it over his head, the RB glistened in the sunlight. "The Renegade Boys is about to take over this shit!"

Chapter 6
Mauricio

Beast and I talked for another twenty minutes before I left his crib to take the two-hour ride to the Danville Correctional facility. I had never been to nobody's mufuckin' jail so I wasn't thrilled to go, but I wanted to confront this nigga about the shit that I had learned. I kept telling myself that I had to practice being calm but that shit wasn't working.

The custody document Beast placed in front of me looked legit as hell, but after he gave me a bank statement with papí's signature on it, I knew at first glance the shit was fake. Big Jim jumped through hoops to knock my father off undetected, and succeeded for years. His ass was in the front pew of the church weeping silently at his funeral and he was the one that put him in the damn casket.

Not to mention this mufucka had a hand in killing my mama. I understood now why he did it, he was a greedy son of bitch. Big Jim wanted to be Reese Williams, but he didn't go about it the right way. He never filled papí's shoes and Big Jim's name didn't get the same reaction as his either. The community didn't love him, they feared him. He didn't make sure the people were straight like papí did, all he did was sold drugs and killed people. His mind was on money and that was all.

My thoughts were consumed from the moment I stepped out of Beast crib to my ride. I didn't think to turn the radio on because the shit I wanted to ask Big Jim took over my mind. Chuckling to myself, I knew his bitch ass wasn't going to fess up to the shit he did, but I knew for a fact the things papí said were true. It didn't really matter what his responses were, he was living on borrowed time. In prison or not, that nigga could be touched.

I pulled into the parking lot of the prison and parked as close as I could to the entrance. Placing my cellphone in the armrest, I took all but a couple dollars out of my pocket. As I got out of my car, I checked my pockets to make sure I didn't have anything illegal on my person.

Looking around at all the barbed wire that surrounded the building, I knew I had to play my cards right because prison was not a place I wanted to be. I wasn't one to be told when I could eat, sleep, or shit. As I got to the door, I paused for a minute because I knew it would be a matter of minutes before I was sitting in front of the nigga that took the two people that I loved dearly away from me.

As I stepped inside, there were a room full of people waiting, I thought I was being smart by coming a little later. There were mainly females with babies that were probably there to see their baby daddies, not knowing the nigga had another bitch and her kids come through on the opposite weekend. That shit was sad, but that's how shit usually played out half the time.

Walking to the window, there was a fine ass, chocolate chick sitting behind the counter looking pretty as hell. She had the smoothest skin that didn't have a scar, bump, or scratch, her face was flawless. Her eyes were dark brown and they almost looked black, kind of demonic like. I looked down at her nametag and it read, Smith.

"May I help you?" She had the prettiest teeth and her neck looked like it needed my lips plastered on the side of it, while I fucked her hard. "Who are you coming to see? Are you gonna stand there staring, or are you gonna tell me who you are here to see, sir?" She sassed with one of her eyebrows raised.

"My bad, Miss Smith. I'm here to see James Carter," I said trying hard to keep my eyes on her face and not on the way the uniform shirt was hugging her big ass titties. They had to be double D's and I could only envision one of her nipples in my mouth.

"I'm going to need your ID, please. And did you make sure your name was on his visitor's list before you made this trip?"

"Yeah, everything is good, ma." I said as I handed her my identification through the small slot in the window.

She was studying it like she was trying to remember the information that was on it. Typing something into the computer, she looked up at me and smiled before she got up and went to the copy machine. Shawty was wearing the fuck out of that uniform, ass was fat for no damn reason. She had a small waist, about five foot seven, maybe one hundred sixty pounds, I would make this drive to see her lil sexy ass every day. I had to have some of that.

"You like what you see? She asked with a smirk on her face.

I couldn't believe she caught me gawking at her body. How long she'd been standing at the window was something I couldn't give the answer to if I was asked. There was a deep dimple that sat in the middle of her left cheek and I envisioned my tongue circling around that mufucka effortlessly.

"Yeah, actually I do. In fact, I'm lovin' it, I'll holla at you before I leave, ma. What time is your shift over?"

"I'm off in two hours, too bad I won't be here when you leave, Mr. Vasquez. By the way, happy birthday," she said with a smile.

"Thank you. What's your name?"

"It sure isn't shawty or ma, it's Latorra."

"Okay Latorra, how about you make my day happier by letting me take you to get something to eat when you get off. Plus, you can help me celebrate my birthday."

"I don't see that happening because I will be long gone by the time you're finished here. Once I clock out, I haul ass."

"Aight," I said nonchalantly.

I'd bet my life her sexy ass would be lurking around when I finished with the chump I was there to see. She was cheesing at a nigga harder than my dick at the moment, only time would tell though. Handing my ID back to me, I signed in and took a seat not too far from her window. After a couple minutes I turned around and sure enough, she was still checking a nigga out.

Twenty minutes later the guards came out to start letting people in for their visits. "I need everyone to line up in a single filed line. Remove everything from your pockets and be prepared to get thoroughly searched. You will have the opportunity to obtain a locker to put your belongings in. Thank you and be patient with us," one of the male guards bellowed as he stated the directions.

I stood in line waiting for my turn to get searched by one of the guards. Low-key I was hoping Latorra would bring her ass from behind the glass and search me personally. Turning to take a peek at her, she was busy signing in more visitors.

"You can step up, sir."

I thought I lucked up and got a female to search me and I was all smiles, but it didn't last long when I saw the guard that was standing waiting for me to step up. The guard had on a uniform just as tight as Miss Smith's and he had an attitude worse than a female.

"We don't have all day to be waiting on you. Either step up or leave, your choice." the guard stated with his hand on his hip.

I almost said something to his sweet ass, but I held my tongue and moved forward. When he started rubbing his hands up my legs, it wasn't a problem. This nigga got to my groin area and I could've sworn he was enjoying the pat down he was doing a little too much. Stepping back before I knocked the fuck out of him, he got the picture when I backed up grilling his ass. He moved the fuck away from me quickly.

Walking to the lockers, I chose one and placed my keys and ID inside and slammed it shut. I walked into the large room that was filled with tables, chairs, and vending machines. I chose a table that was in the back part of the room because the things I wanted to discuss, didn't need to be overheard by the guards. I went to one of the vending machines and bought some snacks so he wouldn't think anything was wrong.

As I was placing the items on the table, the inmates entered the room. Spotting Big Jim as he made his entrance, he was looking around like he was trying to figure out who was there to see him. I took that opportunity and stood up. When he saw me, he smiled and made his way where I was.

"What up, nephew," he said pulling me into a half hug. I hugged him back but that shit was brief. "Happy birthday, nigga. I didn't even know you were coming, all they said was I had a visitor. You and your brothers been on my visitors list since I got here, but this is the first time I've seen you."

This nigga started the visit with a lie falling from his lips. Beast had the warden to check Big Jim's visitors list and neither me nor my brother's names were on it. I guess he was trying to figure out how I got in the prison to see him.

"Thanks for the birthday wish, I wanted to pop in to see how you were holding up," I said with a smirk on my face.

"I'm cool in here. My lawyer is looking into some shit that was mishandled in my case, I may be getting out soon. You know they can't hold a real nigga down in this bitch too long. Damn, you lookin' more and more like yo' daddy, boy," he said laughing.

"You make that shit sound like a bad thing," I said laughing with him. "Speaking of my daddy, I had a talk with him this morning."

Confusion was etched on his face and he started shifting in his seat. He appeared nervous all of a sudden and he had every right to be. My eyes stayed focused on his because I wanted to see just how uncomfortable he was going to get.

"What you talking about, Ricio? Reese been gone four years, man. How the fuck did you have a conversation with him? Did his death have that much of an impact on you?"

"What do you think? Papí died in front of me when I was seventeen years old. Was I supposed to forget about that shit and move on with life? Hell nah, that night would be embedded in my brain forever. But check it, let's discuss the last time *you* talked to him for twenty minutes and fifty-four seconds that same night. See, this shit has been fucking with me mentally and I need answers."

"How do you know I talked to him that day?" he asked curiously.

"I'm asking the questions today, nigga. All I want you to do is answer accordingly. What was the last conversation about when you called his phone?"

"We were talking about business that needed to be handle in the streets. I won't go into the details because you wouldn't understand, youngin. It was grown folk business. Where are you going with this?"

"Not one day after his death did you try to genuinely console me and my brothers, and that bothered me," I stated calmly. "I know more than yo' ass think I do, nigga. You went from taking orders, to dishing them mufuckas out before papí could be embalmed. How the fuck does that happen, James Carter? You put his boys to work on the corner slangin' dope, when you knew first hand that wasn't the life he wanted for us. You hopped on his throne like a hoe on a hard dick, nigga."

"Wait a minute! Are you trying to insinuate I had something to do with Reese going down? If that's what you are implying, I'm done with this visit!" he said loud enough to draw the attention of the guards and some of the visitors too.

I didn't give a fuck because he wasn't getting away that easily. One of the guards was making his way to our table, but that didn't shut me up. "Sit yo' muthafuckin' ass down, nigga! This visit ain't over for another three hours and fifty minutes, or until I say it's over, whichever one comes first!" I growled lowly.

By that time, the guard was standing next to his pussy ass but looking at me. "Everything okay, Carter?" he asked continuing to glare at me.

"Yeah, all is good, Phillips. We just had a slight disagreement, nothing to worry about."

"Keep it down or I'll have to end your visit. You know the rules."

"I already know, I'll keep shit down, my apologies."

The guard looked at both of us and nodded his head before he went back to his post. Big Jim slowly lowered his body into the chair and glanced around the room. Some of the inmates were giving signals to him and he kept holding his hand up and shaking his head no. I wasn't worried about none of them mufuckas, we could tear this bitch up if it came to that.

"I'm not insinuating a damn thing about what I said to you. I heard about what you and Floyd was on from Maurice Williams himself. He got wind of you greedy mufuckas stealing from him. Instead of being his right-hand man that he paid you to be, you decided to come up with a plan to take over his shit. What you didn't know was, he already had yo' ass on his radar. That gave him the opportunity to tell his story from the grave. You even went the extra mile of falsifying custody papers to keep my brothers close so you would have access to what they were to inherit when my mother died. Yep, I know about that shit too, nigga."

When I spoke on my mom, his eyes were big as saucers. The thought of him having something to do with her death was pure speculation, but his reaction let me know he had a hand in it. Sweat was forming on his forehead and it wasn't even hot in the room. He couldn't keep still and his eyes kept shifting back and forth.

"I—I didn't have anything to do with Maritza's death, she was a junkie, Ricio. The only thing I was guilty of was fucking her behind Reese's back. I loved her, nephew. You gotta believe me," he pleaded. "As far as the paperwork, Reese signed those papers and told me to hold on to them."

Shaking my head slowly, I leaned across the table as far as I could, "lie again, bitch! My mother wouldn't fuck with yo' ass if somebody paid her. She didn't even like you, nigga. She was always telling papí to watch you because there was something about you that she couldn't put her finger on. So, for you to sit there and say you were fucking her, nope not believing that shit. She was the queen of our castle and Papí treated her as such. A junkie? My mother didn't like what he did to make money and that shit wasn't allowed in our home. She didn't know the first thing about using drugs, let alone administering that shit into herself with a needle. So, come again, patna. As for the custody papers, that shit was forged! I compared signatures my damn self. Fess up, you needed him gone because you didn't want to walk in his shadow anymore. You wanted to be the kingpin of Chicago, right?"

Big Jim's demeanor changed when he heard me break down the shit I knew. "Ricio, I *am* the kingpin of Chicago, even from behind bars I'm running the city, nigga. Ain't shit yo' ass can do about none of this shit! I guess you've been playing detective since you *college student*. That education shit won't help you in the streets. Don't fuck with me, I can have your ass six feet under with yo' parents if you don't stay outta my business." he said cockily.

"That's the Big Jim I was waiting to see. That bitch nigga that came out first must be the one that's sucking dick around this mufucka. Yo business is my business! You wouldn't have shit if it wasn't for the blood of Reese Williams being on your hands, pussy. I want you to realize something, Big Jim, that same blood runs through my veins. I'm coming for my daddy's throne, get ya army ready. The Renegade Boys take-over is in full effect. I'll be waiting on yo' hoe ass to touch down too, I got something for ya, nigga."

I stood up, pushed the chair close to the table, and made my way to the exit. I was done talking to his ass. If we were anywhere other than the prison, I would've killed him on sight.

"Ricio, get back over here, muthafucka! We got shit to talk about!" he yelled across the room.

"Carter, your visit is over! I've warned you once before." The guard stormed over to him and grabbed his arm. Big Jim fought hard trying to get away from him and that made other guards go over to help restrain him.

"This shit ain't over, nephew!"

Pausing at the door, I turned around so he could see my face. "I'm not yo' nephew, and my daddy wasn't yo' brother either, bitch ass nigga. You started this shit, Big Jim, I'm prepared to finish it."

"Come on so I can get you out of here. You are not allowed back in this prison, I should have your punk ass arrested!" The guard screamed as I walked to the locker that had my belongings in it.

"You don't have to worry about me ever coming back to this mufucka, I promise you that." I said leaving out of the prison.

I stormed out of the prison with a guard on my ass, I went straight for my whip. I felt I'd achieved what I set out to do but I was fuming inside. I already knew that Big Jim was going to clap back, it was just the matter of when he would come for me. I wasn't worried about any of that shit and I had to inform Sosa and execute a plan.

"Do you make a habit of coming to a heavily guarded prison causing a ruckus, Mr. Vasquez?"

I recognized the voice immediately, but I was no longer eager to smile at her. Latorra was walking in my direction as I snatched the driver's door open. The way her thighs were rubbing together with every step she took, I still didn't show any signs of lust. After the encounter I had with Big Jim, the only thing I wanted to do was get away from the Danville Correctional facility.

"Get in, shawty," I said climbing in the seat and motioning to closed the door.

"I can't leave with you—"

"You can and you will. Now stop bullshitting and get in the car, or stand there and watch me roll out. Yo' choice." I said slamming the door closed.

She walked to the passenger side and got in, buckling her seatbelt. "My car is here so you will have to bring me back." She said quietly.

"No problem, I can do that. I don't know anything about this town, where can we go to eat? A nigga starving." I said turning the key in the ignition.

"There's not much out this way, but there is a small bed and breakfast place that allows visitors to go eat. It's about a quarter mile down the road."

Backing out of the spot, I followed the road and the small establishment was sitting alone in the middle of nowhere. They made sure there was nothing remotely close to the prison. If someone escaped, they had nowhere to hide because only open fields could be seen for miles, except Mama's Den. That was the name that displayed on the building. I parked in the front of the entrance and opened my door to get out, Latorra followed suit and led the way inside.

I held the door open for her and she smiled up at me walking inside. As we approached the counter, an older woman came to assist us. "Hello Officer Smith. How are you today? I see you won't be dining alone. Would you like your usual table?"

"I'm doing fine, Mary Jane, thanks for asking. Maybe a table on the patio would be a better choice for us today. Where's Bill?"

"He's in the kitchen cooking today. Jacob's out sick so he had to take his place. You know he's not pleased about it but he didn't have a choice." She laughed grabbing a couple menus and escorted us to the patio. "I'll be back to take your orders, we have your favorite tomato minestrone soup today."

"That's good to know! I will definitely order some." Latorra said excitedly.

"Alright, take your time, I'll be back shortly.

Mary Jane walked away and I was still staring at Latorra. Taking in her features, she was beautiful. The dimple in her cheek appeared the minute she smiled, I fell in love with it all over again. Every time she swiped her hair out of her face and placed the loose strands behind her ear, I couldn't help licking my lips.

"Ummm, are you ready to talk about what happened back at the prison?" she asked cutting into my thoughts.

"Nah, there's nothing to talk about. We can talk about you though, tell me about Latorra Smith." I said looking down at the menu.

"Well, I'm twenty-three years old, I'm from the Southside of Chicago, I've been working at the prison for four months, and I don't have any kids."

"You drive two hours every day to work? Is it worth the drive?"

"It's a job and yes it pays pretty well. I hate the mileage I'm putting on my car, but it pays the bills."

"That's what's important. So, you're from my stomping grounds, huh? You gon' come see a nigga sometime, Miss Smith?" I asked slyly.

"You don't even know if I have a man—"

"I don't give a fuck about yo' man, Latorra. Obviously, he's not on his shit if you're sitting here with me. If your relationship was solid, a nigga wouldn't be able to get a second of your time. Now would you answer the question, ma?"

"How do I know you don't have a woman?" she shot back.

"Now you want to answer a question with a question." I said shaking my head. "You don't know because you didn't ask. I'm a nigga that has nothing to lie about. I have bitches that I fuck with, that's as far as it goes. There's not one female that can call Mauricio Vasquez her man, I'm single."

She looked at me like I had two heads. "That's game if I say so myself Mauricio. Admit it, you are a playa."

"I don't play anyone, shawty. Females play themselves when they think they can force a relationship on me when I've made it clear what it is from the start. I don't make false promises to anyone. The day I stop fuckin' around with multiple women, would be the day someone steals my heart. Right now, I haven't run into that woman. Let me correct that statement, there is one that has the potential to be the one, but I won't subject her to my bullshit."

"So, you are trying to add me to your herd of hoes?"

"I don't have hoes, I have friends with benefits. Latorra, we don't ever have to have sex. If you just want to go out and have a good time, I'm all for that. I just want to get to know you. I'll tell you this though, if you open up and give me the pussy, you would definitely become a friend with benefits. My list of benefits is just that, sexual benefits for me. I don't choose who's in that category, the women do that on their own."

"You are so blunt with it though."

"There's no other way to be. Why put on a façade when you can tell the truth? It's not about how much pussy I can get, it's about who's willing to dish that shit out. I'm real about my mine, ma. Again, will I see you after today?"

Before she could answer, my apple watch started vibrating. I hit the button to connect the call to my Bluetooth. "What up?"

"Happy birthday, Ricio! What are you doing?" Chante asked.

"I'm having lunch with a friend. Thank you for the birthday shout out, but I'll holla at you later."

"Who is the bitch? When are you going to stop fucking around on me, Ricio?"

"For starters, you don't know this woman to call her out of her name. You got the game fucked up, ma. We are not nor have we ever been in a relationship so it's impossible for me to fuck around *on you.* You already know what we have and it's not what you're making it out to be. It's not hard to stop calling. I'm being rude right now, I'll get at you some other time." Not waiting for her to respond, I ended the call.

Mary Jane came back at that moment and took our orders. I decided on the meatloaf, mashed potatoes, and sweet corn. Latorra ordered a steak medium rare, with a baked potato, asparagus, and a bowl of tomato minestrone soup. We both order pink lemonade for our drinks. She was quietly tapping away on her phone with a scowl on her face.

"You good over there?"

Glancing up from her phone, Latorra nodded her head and went back to her phone. I wasn't about to pry into whatever was on her mind, if she wanted to tell me what was going on, she would. While waiting for our food and Latorra to finish whatever she was doing, I decided to text Sosa.

Me: Aye bro, I need to meet up with you as soon as I get back to the city. All I can say is I had a conversation with Beast, and I went to see Big Jim. I'll hit you up to see where you at. Have your brother there too, both of you need to hear what I have to say."

Sosa: Bet

Latorra finally placed her phone on the table, folding her hands. "Mauricio, I'm a one-man woman. I don't think trying to be more than friends would work for me. Developing a friendship is fine with me. The way you had to explain yourself to whomever called you, only tells me that your flock is vicious. I don't do well with disrespect."

"I understand, ma. Just know, all their asses get checked if they get out of pocket. There's no reason for anyone to get mad about anything I do because I don't belong to nobody." I said reaching across the table for her phone.

I pushed the button to add my number to her contacts and I had access. She didn't try to stop me so I knew then that she wanted my number. After I inserted my number, I slid the phone back to her. Mary Jane came out with our food and I was ready to smash, I was hungry as hell. She placed my plate of meatloaf in front of me and the aroma hit my nose. The growling of my stomach was loud.

"Somebody is hungry." Mary Jane said with a chuckle.

"I am. This food smells delicious, thank you."

"Well let me know if you all need anything else. We have homemade strawberry cheesecake for dessert, just to let you know. Enjoy your meal." She said walking away.

Mary Jane was so nice and I was going to leave her a nice tip for her great customer service. I said a silent prayer and raised my head. My eyes connected with Latorra's and she had a huge smile on display.

"What?" I asked.

"I don't see many men who pray anymore. I was shocked, that's all."

"Real niggas pray too, ma. When you're raised right, some things carry on over into your daily routine no matter what type of life you live. If nobody else has got my back, I know I can count on the Man Upstairs."

I cut into the meatloaf and put a piece into my mouth, it was delectable. I hadn't had a meatloaf this good since my mama passed away. Even though she was Dominican, she loved cooking soul food and I missed everything about her. Cutting another piece, I added some mashed potatoes to the fork and damn near cried. It was as if she came down and cooked this meal specially for me. It was a taste I could never forget. It was a must for me to take more with me for later.

"You alright over there?" Latorra asked quietly.

"Yeah, this meatloaf tastes just like my mama's. It brought back memories."

"Tell me about her?"

"That's a story for another day. I'm already appearing soft around you as it is." I chuckled.

"There's nothing soft about you, Mauricio. I can tell you are a piece of work." She laughed while cutting into her steak.

"You got jokes, huh?"

"Tell me about Mauricio Vasquez. What do you do for a living? I know you have a woman for every day of the week, do you have siblings?"

"I do not have a woman for every day of the week, maybe two." I laughed. "Nah, for real though, it's not as it seems. I'm a business man and work a lot so, I don't have that much time on my hands. My brothers and I was born and raised on the south side. My parents raised us well until they passed away four years ago. Stepping up to make sure we were good in their absence was something I had to do."

"I'm sorry to hear that. I have to be honest with you, I thought you were a street guy."

"What, you got something against street niggas or something?" I asked putting another piece of meatloaf in my mouth.

"I've had my share of street guys and that world could lead to two places, jail or the grave. Plus, the streets are more important to them than anything. That's just my opinion."

"Sounds to me like you're used to fuckin' with fuck boys. You have to broaden your horizons. All street niggas are not the same. We all in the same game, just on different levels. Dealing with the same hell, with different devils. But you wouldn't understand any of that Miss CO. A real man would know how to make time for his woman, regardless of what he has going on."

"You are living the street life, huh? I see my assumption was spot on and you're right, I would never understand. Let me guess, you are a worker."

"I don't know you like that to let you know my level of operation. Are you ready to get out of here?" I asked.

"Change the subject why don't you" she chuckled. "Yes, I'm ready. It was nice meeting you, Mr. Vasquez. Thank you for lunch and the great conversation."

"My pleasure, beautiful." I said as I waved Mary Jane over for the check.

She walked over with the biggest smile on her face. "Did you guys enjoy your meal?"

"Yes, we did. The meatloaf was delicious, it tasted just like my mother's. I would like to have two of the meatloaf meals to go please." I said reaching into my pocket pulling out two one hundred-dollar bills.

"This is too much! I'll bring your change and meals to go shortly." She held one of the bills out to me and I shook my head no repeatedly.

"Take it, Mary Jane. That is for your great customer service, thank you. Keep the change."

"Thank you, sir. Come inside and I'll go ahead and get your order together."

Standing from the chair that I was sitting in, I watched Latorra gather her belongings and I knew I had to have her. She was going to call a nigga soon because I could see the curiosity in her eyes. I pushed the chair in and held out my hand for her to grasp. She looked at me and wrapped her hand around my arm instead and I led her into the building.

"Did you want anything to take home with you?" I asked looking down at her.

"The cheesecake sounds delicious. I'll have a piece of that to go."

We went to the counter and Mary Jane was bagging up someone's food. There were so many bags. Whoever that order was for had a huge family and they didn't want to cook. Even the cheesecake was boxed up ready to go. Looking over at Latorra, she had a frown on her face, I guess because we missed out on her getting a piece. I'll just have to take her to the Cheesecake Factory someday and let her eat her heart out.

"I'm almost finished packing your order, give me a sec." Mary Jane said glancing up from what she was doing.

When she walked over with the bags of food, I was shocked. She had packed all the food for me. I guess taking the money as a tip was something her pride wouldn't allow her to do. I wanted to protest but I knew she wasn't going to let me decline.

"You didn't have to do this, Mary Jane."

"I know I didn't. I haven't seen anyone as genuine about my cooking as you. I couldn't let you give me that large of a tip without showing my appreciation." She smiled.

"Would you do me a favor and put two slices of the cheesecake in a separate container for the lady?" I nodded my head toward Latorra.

"I don't need to do that, she has her own right over there." Mary Jane motioned behind her as she placed the bags on the counter and turned to retrieve the others.

"Thank you so much, Mary Jane." Latorra said excitedly.

The amount of food Mary Jane packed was more than the two hundred dollars I had given her. I spotted a tip jar on the counter. Digging in my pocket, I peeled off several bills and dropped them inside.

"Damn balla." Latorra said looking at me.

"Nah, she's giving me food that she could've made money from. I'm not trying to let her do that. I love her hospitality, but she has a business to run."

"That was nice of you. You not really from the Southside, are you? Those niggas would've taken the food without looking back."

"I was born and raised on the Southside, there's only one Mauricio Vasquez, I can't be duplicated, ma. You'll see if you hang with the kid long enough."

Once we had all the bags, I thanked Mary Jane again and made our way to the car. When I pulled back into the prison parking lot, the anger reemerged. If I go inside and see Big Jim again, I'd kill his ass, but his day was coming.

"What are you in deep thought about?" Latorra asked cutting into my thoughts.

"Nothing for you to worry about. Let me help you with these bags." I said getting out of the car.

I got the bags out of the backseat and waited for her to unlock her doors. She opened the backdoor of her Toyota Malibu and I placed them on the floor of her car. When I turned around, she wrapped her arms around my waist. The scent of her perfume filled my nostrils.

"Thanks again for lunch. I'll give you a call soon. Happy birthday again."

"Thank you, don't have me waiting too long for you to reach out to me." I said letting her go.

I held the door open so she could get in and closed it once she was settled. She started the car and let the window down. "Drive carefully, sexy. I'll be waiting to hear from you." I smiled, tweaking her cheek.

Walking around to my car, I was ready to get back to the city to spring this news on Sosa. I hoped Max didn't come through on bullshit because he was not exempt from getting his ass kicked. Latorra backed out of the parking spot and I followed her to the highway. I thought about her the entire time I was driving. She was definitely someone I wanted to spend some time with.

***

I arrived home two hours later and immediately took a shower. As I pulled on a fresh pair of boxers, my phone chimed with a text. Grabbing it from the dresser I opened it and there was an unknown number displayed. With a frown on my face, I opened the text and smiled.

(773) 555-0711: I'm home safely. I figured I'd text since you didn't ask for my number. Enjoy the rest of your birthday, Mr. Vasquez.

Me: Thank you, ma. I'm glad you made it home. I'm taking care of some business, I'll holla at you later.

I locked Latorra's number into my phone after returning the text. She'd reached out faster than expected, but I had plans for her cute ass. Walking to the closet to find an outfit to wear, I skimmed through my gear and decided on a pair of black True Religion jeans, the matching black button down, and my black Timbs. I took my black fitted cap from the hat box and laid everything on the bed.

Once I was dressed, I grabbed my chain and put it around my neck. I picked up my phone and hit Sosa's name and waited for him to pick up. His phone went to voicemail and I was about to try again when my phone started ringing. It was him calling back.

"What up, bro? I'm on my way to yo' crib. Did you get in touch with Max's punk ass?"

"Yeah, he is on his way over now. I didn't tell him you were coming, I just told him that I needed to talk to him about something. Ricio, I understand what he did was wrong, but that's still our bro. Can you just squash this shit?" he asked.

"I didn't ask for him to be there so there'd be beef. The shit I have to say is important and shit is about to change for all of us. I want him to know the people that he's riding for is

82

not what they seem. But I will get into that when I get there. I'm leaving out of my crib now. I should be there in a half hour."

"Aight, see you when you get here. Love."

I grabbed my keys and left out the door. As I was waiting on the elevator to come, the thought of how quiet my place was without Nija there had me bugging. It felt cozy when Nija spent time over because she cooked and we chilled. But when it was just me alone, I felt like I was being smothered by the silence that floated around. That was part of the reason I didn't spend a lot of time in my own place, it wasn't quite a home. One day that would change and I would have plenty of baby Mauricio's running around. Until then, I had to live with the way things were for now.

I got to the garage and jumped in my whip. Driving to Sosa's crib on the far south side, I was banging Kendrick Lamar's *Damn* album. The track "Humble" was one that I could listen to all day. As I pulled up into Sosa's driveway, the first thing I saw was Max's Charger parked next to Sosa's BMW. I parked behind Sosa's whip because I knew if my little brother got out of pocket, I was going to have to lay hands on him. His punk ass wouldn't think twice about backing his shit into mine to get out.

I sat in the car for a bit before I turned off the ignition and got out. Using my key, I let myself inside. The voices of Sosa and Max could be heard coming from the dining room area. When I stepped into the room, Max glanced up and the smile that he wore, quickly changed to a grimace. My little brother had never looked at me that way before. That was an indication that Big Jim and Floyd was all in his ear with bullshit.

"Sosa, you didn't tell me this nigga was coming over here. I'm out." He said standing up from the chair that he was sitting in.

"I didn't come over to discuss that bullshit that happened yesterday! We already established what the fuck went down with that. What I have to say is way more important than the little shit you pulled, Max. I need to tell you about the muthafucka that you are idolizing over papí."

"I'm not putting nobody over Papí. Big Jim was there when he was taken away from us, what the fuck you mean?" he snapped.

"Nigga, Big Jim is the reason Papí ain't here! I found out a lot of shit today and that nigga a snake. He was the one behind both of our parents dying!"

"Hold the fuck up, Ricio. What the fuck did you just say?" Sosa asked.

"You heard me right, brah. That muthafucka was the one that put the hit on Papí."

"Where did you get that bullshit from? Whoever the fuck is running Big Jim's name through the mud is getting dealt with! That's a violation and I won't let that shit slide!" Max yelled.

I looked at his ass like he had a herpes bump on his lip. He was talking tough and once again jumping to that pussy ass nigga's defense. The shit was making me madder with every word that fell from his lips.

"I'm waiting, Mauricio. Tell me who the muthafucka is that told you that shit! Big Jim has been there for us from the day papí died! Even though Big Jim got popped, he's still looking out for us from behind them walls. We still eating nigga! But you want to go off word of a muthafucka that's probably jealous!"

Shaking my head at Max, I had to take a deep breath before I reached out and choked the fuck out of his stupid ass. I had to coach myself into staying calm because when it was all said and done, that was still my brother. The way he was coming to this nigga's defense was getting to me because I heard all the cocky shit he said with my own ears. I couldn't get the fact that Big Jim lied on my mama out of my head either. Not to mention, he killed my mufuckin' daddy.

"I'm waiting for you to tell me who the fuck told you that bold faced lie, Ricio." Max said continuing to run off at the mouth.

"Everything I said came from a reliable source. That nigga has been living foul off Papi! The way he came up was because he took out the Big Fish to get the spot at the top. Maurice Williams died because James Carter wanted to be "the man" in Chicago!"

"Okay, Ricio hold on. Start from the beginning because since the day Papi died, I knew something was fishy about a lot of shit." Sosa said directly to me.

Walking into the kitchen, I pulled a glass tumbler from the cabinet along with a bottle of Hennessy and poured a shot. After I downed it, I went back to the table and stood with my arms folded. There was so much that needed to be said, I didn't know where to start.

"Last night after the shit happened between me and Max, I called Beast to tell him to talk to the lil nigga—"

"You was the reason his ass called me talking shit! I'm not a kid no more, Ricio, can't nobody tell me—"

"Shut the fuck up!" both me and Sosa screamed at the same time.

"I'm not trying to hear that shit right now, somebody needed to tell yo' ass something before I put my foot in your ass! For the record, this man right here, is the reason yo' ass ain't beat for pulling ya gun on me!" I said pointing at Sosa.

"Man, I'm not about to sit here and listening to this shit. Yo' muthafuckin' ass is jealous of Big Jim and I don't know why. You need to get ya shit together and stop trying to bite the hand that's been making a way to feed yo' ass all these years. If it wasn't for him, you wouldn't have shit!"

Max brushed past me and headed for the door. I followed behind him and Sosa was behind me. He reached out to open the door and my words stopped him in his tracks. "That nigga stopped our father from breathing and yo' ass won't listen to what the fuck I have to say to bring the shit to light! You dancing with the devil, stupid ass! That muthafucka killed papí and forged papers to get custody of you and Sosa. Mama mysteriously died of a drug overdose but she never even drank wine. Nigga, that shit was a setup! Big Jim eliminated both of them and you riding with this nigga!"

"I don't give a fuck what you say! Like I said, whoever told you that shit is lying!" he said snatching the door open.

Before he could step foot outside the door, I grabbed him by the back of his neck and flung him back inside. The first thing he did was reached for his waistband and I punched him in the side of his face with all my might. I was not giving him the opportunity to up another pistol on me. Sosa stepped in between us at the moment Max was swinging back at me, hitting Sosa in the back of the head.

"Max, I will fuck you up!" Sosa said standing toe to toe with him. "Y'all aint about to tear my crib up! I don't know what your problem is, but you need to check yo'self. We ain't yo enemies, Max. I believe what Ricio is saying and I think you should hear him out."

"I don't believe nothing his ass is saying. I can live my own life, I was doing fine while y'all was away at school getting y'all education on and shit. Big Jim taught me how to get money and learn to survive in these streets! All y'all wanna do is tell me what not to do, it's too late for that shit."

"So, surviving is pulling a gun every time you feel threatened?" I asked. "If that's what you call survival, baby brah, you are in a world of trouble. Yo' ass is gon' pull that piece on the wrong mufucka and I hate to say you're not gon' live to tell about it."

"Fuck both of y'all!"

Sosa punched his ass in the mouth because he talked too fuckin' much. I don't know why he thought his ass couldn't get dealt with for the disrespect. Max tried swinging back but he was not ready for the technical training that Sosa was delivering to his ass. I could tell he wasn't trying to hurt Max, but he was proving to him that he wasn't about that life.

With every blow Sosa hit him with, he could only bring one back in return. His punches weren't fazing Sosa at all. When the blood started oozing out of Max's mouth from the uppercut Sosa delivered to his chin, I knew I had to stop the beat down.

"Aight, brah, that's enough." I said pulling Sosa back by his arm. He snatched away and punched Max in his jaw and he fell in a heap on the floor. "Eso es suficiente, Sosa!" (That's enough Sosa!) I repeated loudly in Spanish.

"Disrespect anyone else in this family and you will get yo' ass beat again! Nunca debes dar la espalda a la familia (You are never supposed to turn your back on family!) I can't force you to stay here and listen to what Ricio found out, but once you walk out that door, I'm done with you."

Max stood up and wiped his mouth on his sleeve, trying to stop the blood from falling on the floor. "Who is this person that told you all of this reliable information?" he asked staring at me.

"It was Papí. I heard everything from Papí's mouth."

"This is what I mean about y'all, always trying to fuck up my head and manipulate me. If this is your way of trying to keep me away from the crew, save it. I already know who I'm down with and that's Big Jim. How the fuck you hear something from somebody that's been dead for years? Get the fuck outta here with that bullshit. I'm out. Keep that psychic shit to ya'self, I don't believe in ghosts." He said rushing out the house to his car.

"Max wait!" I yelled out, but he kept going.

"Let his ass go, I need you to fill me in on what the fuck is going on. I'll go talk to his ass later. If I have all the information, I can make him see things your way, but you have to tell me everything." Sosa said heading to the basement as I watched Max speed up the street.

Chapter 7
Maximo

Speeding away from Sosa's house, I was on ten. I couldn't believe my own brothers tried to pull that sucker shit with me. There was no way I was going against the grain. Big Jim had been the reason I was eating in these streets. He taught me how to hustle to make money and I kept a lot of it in my pockets.

At eighteen years old, I'd finished high school and didn't have to wait two weeks to get paid at nobody's workplace. All I had to do was beat the block and watch out for the police. The crew that Floyd and Big Jim had was loyal and I trusted them to watch my back.

The shit that Ricio said pissed me off because I knew Big Jim was thorough. When Ricio said he was the one that set my father up, I wasn't staying around to listen to them slaughter his character. I had to ask three times who the source was that told them that bullshit. The best answer he could come up with was, he heard it from my father's mouth. That was impossible because he was not among the living anymore.

I parallel parked my ride in a spot that sat directly in front of the trap I was in charge of and got out. Shake, John John, and Red was serving rocks like candy. The fiends were out and about copping their poison of choice. Business was good as usual and I was ready to get in on this money.

"What up Max? Where the hell you been?" Red asked as he completed a transaction and walked beside me to the porch.

"I had some shit that I needed to take care of. I see there's lots of money out here tonight."

"Hell yeah, I'm working on my fourth pack. I'm about to ride out though, this hoe I met at the club Saturday tryin' to get up. You know I'm not passin' up no pussy, nigga!" Red said laughing.

"Go handle ya' business while I get in on this check. Make sure yo' ass strap up because these bitches are treacherous out here. Beautiful, bodied up, and low-key got that package. Muthafuckin' dick fall off in yo' hand fuckin' with these hoes."

"Shid, he'd better watch out for those too pretty bitches, fuck around and have a dick in *his* mouth!" John John blurted out from the porch.

We all laughed at that shit, except Red of course. "Nigga, that shit ain't funny. I wish a muthafucka would pull that shit on me. It would be the last time his ass pulled a stunt like that because they would be looking for his ass for a very long time. Come up missing playing that gay shit with me."

"Why is yo' ass getting all sensitive about the subject, man? You know we just jokin' and shit." I said still laughing.

"He's pissed off because Genesis almost tricked his ass at club Odyssey that one time. I gotta give it to her ass though, she was fine as hell. But he didn't peep that Adam's apple like I did." Shake laughed. "As a matter of fact, nigga, you still owe me for that shit."

I laughed so hard at the way Red was looking. His face matched his name at that moment. He was embarrassed as hell, I guess that was a secret that wasn't supposed to come out. The mean mug he threw at Shake was priceless.

"Fuck you! I peeped that shit, get the fuck outta hear with that shit! Man, I'm out." Red said storming to his ride.

"Man, Shake, why you put him on blast like that?" I asked jogging up the steps to sit on the porch.

"He needs to slow his ass down. Every pretty bitch he see he's trying to get at. Thirsty ass always splurging on these hoes to get some pussy. Enough about that nigga, what's up with yo' brother, Max?"

I didn't know which one of my brother's Shake was referring to but I knew it wasn't good from the way he said that shit. "What you mean, fam?"

"I got a call from Floyd a couple hours ago and he wasn't happy. He got a call from Big Jim today. Mauricio went to the prison to pay him a visit and he was mad disrespectful. He was in there throwing accusations around, calling big homie all kinds of shit. Claiming he got word that Big Jim is the one that laid yo' Pops down."

I didn't say anything because I needed to know what else he had to say. I didn't give Ricio the opportunity to tell me what he wanted to talk about, I was in the dark. It was hard for me to believe Big Jim had anything to do with the shit he was speaking on because he looked out for a nigga.

"I don't know shit about none of that. I'm not fuckin' with Ricio right now, fuck him and Sosa. Them niggas don't give a fuck about me, blood don't make you related, loyalty does. I'm good on them right now. I don't know where the fuck he could've gotten that shit from but he needs to slow his roll. It's not a good look to be throwing niggas under the bus like that."

"Well Floyd wants to holla at his ass. I tried calling him but he ain't answering none of my calls. He knows that he fucked up and dodging a nigga. He didn't come see Floyd to give his take from the trap on 26th street and you know that's a mandatory task. I need you to hit his line and tell that nigga to get at Floyd, Asap!"

"I just told you I'm not fuckin' with them niggas. Don't come at me with the bullshit they on because it ain't got shit to do with me. Whatever they got going on, don't involve me. My money's straight with Big Jim."

"I'm letting you know they need to turn that money in because we don't do that stealing shit around these parts. On top of that, he disrespected the head nigga in charge while he's on lock! He knew Big Jim couldn't touch his ass but that's what his crew is for in these streets, to have his muthafuckin' back! Yo' brother don't want to go to war with us, his army is our army and we stand strong together. He is outnumbered. I suggest you holla at that nigga and let him know, this is not what he wants." Shake snared.

"Damn Shake, you don't have to come at my brother like that, nigga. What is you not saying? It got to be more to the story if you heated like that. I don't think he's trying to rip y'all off, so you can quit saying that shit. We wasn't raised to take shit from nobody. Ricio and Sosa work hard in these streets just like yo' ass. I may be beefing with him, but what you won't do is try to shit on his character."

"I know what I was told and the way he came at the Boss. Mauricio's on bullshit."

"Tell me what the fuck was said and maybe we can figure this shit out together." I said trying to get him to say more.

"Nah, this don't involve you, remember? I'll wait to talk to that nigga when the time presents itself. Until then, get over there and give those hypes what they need to take that monkey off their backs." He said sitting in the chair next to me.

I stood up and walked down the stairs. There were two fiends walking up the walkway. "Let me get five young blood." One of them said. Handing him what he asked for, I took the money and put it in my pocket. That's the way business went for the next two hours, steady. Shake had me thinking about the shit he'd said and I had a feeling shit was about to get real. He didn't elaborate on what was said between Ricio and Big Jim, but from the little bit I gathered from Ricio, something wasn't right.

Shake had left about an hour after our conversation, leaving me and John John to work the block. He wasn't selling shit so I knew he was there to keep an eye on me for whatever reason. I didn't give a fuck because in that short time, I got off three packs and my pockets were sitting pretty. I took my phone out and shot Ricio a text.

Me: Aye, you need to hit up Floyd or Shake they looking for you.

I laid my phone in my lap to wait for his reply. When my phone vibrated, I looked at the screen and it was my girlfriend Madysen. "What's up baby?" I spoke into the phone.

"Where you at, Max? I've been waiting on you to call me all day."

"I'm out getting this money. Don't start this shit today Mads, I got enough shit to worry about. The last thing I need is for you to start that hounding shit."

"Well if you would pick up the phone and say hello throughout the day, I wouldn't do it."

"Yo' ass lying. The only thing you want me to do is check in because you think I'm with a bitch. Ya' mind on the wrong shit, ma. I can't be out here in the streets with a phone up to my ear, that's how a nigga get caught slipping. I'm hanging up and I'll be over later. Have my girl ready for me, aight?"

"Whatever, Max." she said hanging up.

Madysen has been on the same shit for the entire two years that we'd been dating. She had every reason to be suspicious of me being unfaithful, I've done plenty of shit with other bitches. She knew about everything and she still chose to be with me. She should be questioning herself, not me, I'm only doing what she allowed me to do. As long as she continued to sit back without speaking on the shit I did, I was going to keep moving accordingly. My phone started vibrating and I looked at the screen and there was a text from Ricio. Opening it up I read what it said.

Ricio: I'm not hard to find but I'll be seeing them niggas soon. Get the fuck away from them Max. If you would have heard me out, you wouldn't be guessing right now. I'm still willing to fill you in, but it won't be over the phone. Feel free to come back to bro's crib, I'll be here for a minute. Under no circumstances are you to give any information on where we lay our heads at night! They ain't for you, bro. Take my word on that shit!

Me: I'm not coming over there tonight. I need time to think about how y'all came at me. Whatever is going on, leave me out of it.

He didn't waste any time responding back to me.

Ricio: Nigga you was born in this shit! Anything that has to do with Maurice Williams is on their radar! Yo' stupid ass will learn the hard way! Get at me so you won't be running around with blinders on and get caught up! Listen for once in your life!

There he was trying to play the big brother role again, I wasn't trying to hear that shit. I didn't attempt to respond to his last message. I was still mad about what transpired in the past couple of days. I'd get with him on another day, it just wouldn't be at that time.

"Aight John John, I'm outta this bitch. I'll holla at ya later." I said dapping him up.

"Where you off to?" he asked looking down the street.

"I'm heading over to Madysen's crib so she can stop trippin' and shit. You already know how she is, man." I said walking down the steps.

"Aye, you talked to your brother?" he asked standing up.

"Nah, I texted him but he didn't respond." I said when I turned around. They were on Ricio hard as fuck. Maybe I did need to go holla at that nigga and get the full story. "I'll make sure to let him know that y'all looking for him when I do hear from him. Be easy, fam." I said heading to my whip.

As I neared the driver's side, a fiend named Slim walked up and I sold him my last three bags. "Hey young blood, watch yourself out here, shit ain't all it seems to be. Take it from me, I've been out here a long time and I respected yo' daddy. Remember, snakes move in silence and attack when you least expect it." he said and walked off.

I didn't know what he meant by that but it had me thinking hard. I opened the door to my whip and decided to go back to Sosa's crib. Stopping at the stoplight, I shuffled through my playlist on my phone to find some music to listen to. I settled on the Todays R&B and Hip-Hop station on Pandora. Prodigal Sunn's "Betrayal" blasted through the speakers. *Keep your eyes on your back, and your face on your stacks. Some living for the lie, while others die for the game. You catch these slugs, engraved with your name.* First Mauricio, then Slim, now an unknown source was trying to tell me something. I needed to pay attention to all the signs. The light changed as I placed the phone in the cup holder.

As I merged onto I-290, I glanced in the rearview mirror and saw a black SUV a couple cars behind me. It looked like Shake's truck but I wasn't sure. When I changed lanes, so did the truck. Driving as normal as possible, I signaled to get over so I could get on the Dan Ryan expressway. Heading southbound, the truck was still tailing me. I decided to get off the expressway at 39th and hit Madysen's crib. When I signaled to get over to make my exit, the SUV did the same. At that moment, I knew I was being followed.

I pulled in front of Madysen's building and parked my ride. The SUV kept going down the street and I was certain it was Shake. I got a good look at his license plate. I just didn't know the point of him following me. Going straight to Madysen's spot was a wise choice because in my mind, I knew they were hoping I led them to my brother.

Getting out, I walked to the door and rang her bell repeatedly. "Who the fuck is it?" Madysen screamed into the intercom.

"It's me babe, open up." I said looking around to make sure nobody was sneaking up on my ass.

The door buzzed releasing the lock and I hurriedly went inside. As I took the steps two at a time to the third floor, the words Slim spoke invaded my thoughts. For the life of me I couldn't put together exactly what he was trying to tell me. Making a mental note to holla at him and find out what he knew, as I walked down the hall.

Madysen was standing with the door open when I walked up. She looked sexy as hell without trying with her little booty shorts, a tight fitted tank, and a pair of fuzzy house shoes on her feet. I loved this girl but she needed to stop nagging me.

"Why were you ringing my bell like that, Max?" She asked closing the door behind me.

"I gotta shit, my bad." I said rushing to the bathroom.

I didn't have to use the bathroom at all. A nigga was nervous and needed answers. Mauricio said he didn't want to discuss anything over the phone but I had to see what was up. Shake wasn't following me for nothing, they were out for blood. I pulled my phone off my hip and pressed on Ricio's name. Waiting for him to pick up, I started biting my nails. That was something I hadn't done since my parents died.

"What up, Max?" his voice boomed through the phone.

"Bro, what the fuck going on? I was on my way to y'all but I had to make a detour to Madysen's crib because Shake was following me. Did you call them?"

"Hell nawl, I didn't call them niggas. They gon' *see* me!"

"Shake making it seem like you stole from them, tell me you ain't trying to take their money, Ricio." I said nervously.

"Nigga are you serious? You ain't never known me to take shit that didn't belong to me. They gon' get their money then I'm done with them mufuckas, and you are too."

"Ricio, I don't have shit to do with whatever beef y'all got going on. Their problem is with you, not me. I gotta get this money, bro. I can't stop doing this shit, a regular job is not for me. This fast money—"

"Shut the fuck up! You saying too much over these airwaves. Are you staying with Madysen tonight?"

"I wasn't planning on staying here, why?"

"Sit tight for the night. I'm making plans to pay them niggas a visit and I don't want you out in these streets. You should've stayed and listened Max, but I will fill you in, I promise. But listen to me bro, stay away from Floyd and the rest of the crew. They are about to gun for us hard with the information I laid on Big Jim. I need you to lay low for me, okay?"

"I hear you, Ricio. I will stay here, but you have to tell me everything."

"Don't worry, I will. Keep your phone on. As a matter of fact, in an hour, I want you and Madysen to leave her crib for the night. Go to a hotel downtown or some shit, they know where you are. Wait for my call because you are gon' have to come to my crib until we can get you another spot. Shit is about to get hot, brah."

"I'm not understanding any of this, man. Why I can't go to my own crib?"

"They know where you lay yo' head! Yo' ass still live in Big Jim's shit! I can't say anything else because we on the phone. Just do what I say and stop asking questions. If yo' hot headed ass would've listened, you would already know what the fuck is going on! In one hour, get the fuck outta there!" he said hanging up the phone.

Chapter 8
Big Jim

As I was escorted back to my cell, I was mad as fuck. Mauricio had heart like his daddy and he came at me like a boss. There hadn't been a nigga that had the balls to speak to me the way he did in years. I loved the challenge though. The plans were forming in my head with every step I took back to the unit. His bitch ass spooked me with the shit he'd said, that was shit I thought died when Reese's bitch ass stopped breathing.

Yeah, I had that nigga's wig pushed back. It was because of the way he constantly came at me like I was his bitch. Reese fed me good, don't get me wrong. But I felt I wasn't getting what I was rightfully due. Working my ass off in the streets of Chicago for his ass and he was the one reaping a bigger chunk of the muthafuckin' benefits.

Reese was living the life I wanted and he was preventing me from getting there. About six months before I took his life, he came to me and we were chilling when he told me he was getting out of the game. That was music to my ears because I knew that he was passing the shit down to me. I had been his right-hand man and knew how to run his operation just like he taught me. I was the nigga in charge when he took his family on vacation for weeks at a time. It was me that was putting the product in the hands of the workers. The only thing I didn't know was who the connect was.

"I'm tired of this shit, Big. I have enough money to live my best life out here. I'm getting out, nigga. My kids are getting older and I want them to make something out of themselves. Getting them prepared for this fucked up world is what I want to do without having to watch my back. I want to be here to enjoy the grandbabies that I know will be coming sooner than later."

"What are you trying to say, Reese. Stop beating around the bush, nigga." I said sipping the cognac I poured minutes before his arrival.

"I'm done, Big. I'm getting out of the game."

"What the fuck is going to happen to the mufuckas that's been riding with you all these years? Reese I've been in your corner from day one."

"Calm yo ass down, Big. I'm gon' front you enough bricks to help you get this money on yo' own. How you maintain that shit is all on you. I think you would be able to make a name for yourself without me. I'll keep you posted on shit once I get everything together. You won't have to worry about shit for a minute anyway. I got you though."

I wasn't about to sit back watching him continue to make money out the ass and I was still struggling with what I was making. The way I was splurging on shit was the reason my money wasn't sitting high, but Reese did the same shit without a worry in the world. That's how I wanted to live my life so I started skimming off the nigga's money and product. He had so much money that he didn't know the shit was missing, so I thought.

Mauricio came in dropping shit in my lap that he couldn't possibly know about and it had me wondering if Reese really told him. How though, was what I needed to find out. When I reached my cell, my cellie was chilling in the top bunk. I needed his ass to get the fuck out so I could make a few calls without him hearing what I was talking about.

"Yo, homie. Go watch tv or something, I got some shit I gotta do in here for a minute." I said as I walked in.

"Damn BJ, I was resting for a minute, a nigga tired."

"What the fuck I tell you about calling me that bullshit? My name is Big Jim, nigga. Do I look like a little ass boy running around this muthafucka? Get the fuck out!"

He scrambled to get down and hurried out the door. I got my phone out of my hiding spot and dialed up Floyd. When he answered I heard his ass moan in the phone and a slurping sound in the background. "Nigga, pull yo' dick from between that bitch's cheeks! We got some shit to talk about now!"

"Damn, Big hold on, I'm almost there!" he moaned in the phone.

"I don't have time for this shit! Tell that hoe to pause and get the fuck up! When I'm finished with yo' ass you can resume that shit. Right now, that's not a top priority!"

"Aaaaarrrrgghh, yeah."

His ass didn't listen for shit! I couldn't be mad because I don't think I would've been able to stop a bitch from making me pop my top on command either. Putting the phone down, I waited five minutes before I picked it back up. I heard the female in the background trying to figure out who was on the phone.

"Who the fuck is it, Floyd?"

"Get the fuck out, Donna! I have business to discuss. As a matter of fact, go in there and cook me something to eat before I slap the fuck outta yo' ass. I don't know how many times I gotta tell you about questioning me!"

A door slammed before he got back on the phone. "Big you there, man? My bad for that. You caught me at a bad time."

"Fuck all that! Mauricio just left and he knows about the mission. He knows shit that he ain't supposed to know, you haven't been running your mouth, have you?"

"I know damn well you didn't just ask me that shit, Big! Me saying something would be equivalent with me telling on my damn self! I'm gon' need you to calm the fuck down and tell me what's up."

"You know I can't tell you everything over this phone. Is that nigga current on payments?"

"Nah, he hasn't brought his money in from his load for the week. Should I be worried?" he asked.

"I don't know where his mind is right now. Call that nigga and tell him to bring my money. Keep yo' eyes open because he was in here like a replica of Reese. His ass was disrespectful as fuck but the shit he knew, he claimed he heard from his daddy. I think the lil nigga's going crazy but the shit he talked about was on point."

"I got this out here, Big. Don't worry about shit. I will lay his ass down if I need to, give the word. I'm about to call this nigga and see what's up, I'll call you back."

"Okay, cool. Get at me." I said ending the call.

I laid back on my bunk and closed my eyes and opened them quickly. The image of Reese was front and center and I hadn't seen that shit since the first week after me killing him. He stalked my black ass for months in my sleep but I knew he couldn't do anything to me from where he was.

I took my tablet from under my pillow and put on some music so I could think. My lawyer had to get shit moving on my case so I could get the hell out of this prison. It's been damn near a year and I wanted out. I'd polluted the streets with crack, but I got knocked for hitting a nigga upside his head. It wasn't my fault the nigga was too weak to take a punch and died. I was protecting myself, it's called self-defense.

Listening to Tupac's "Only God Can Judge Me", thinking about all the shit that I had endured in my life. I let my eyes close waiting on Floyd to get back to me. I don't know how long I had been laying there but I felt my phone vibrate on the side of me. I grabbed it and saw that it was damn near eight o'clock and Floyd was just calling back.

"What up?" I said in a low tone. I didn't have long to talk because the guards would be in to count soon. The last thing I needed was to get caught on this phone.

"I've been calling Mauricio since I got off the phone with you and he's still not answering. I went by the trap on 26th and they haven't seen him all day. When I asked about Sosa, they said they hadn't seen him either. With that being said, he still hasn't been through with yo' paper. Shake and John John saw Max earlier but he said something about him and his brothers beefing. He's not fucking with them at all right now."

"Use that nigga to get to them. He is gullible as hell and he will fall right into the trap. As a matter of fact, I'll hit him up myself. He still looks up to a nigga, unlike his punk ass brother."

"Shake followed him when he left the trap on Independence, but he went to his broad crib over on 39th and Calumet. Shake was hoping he led him to Ricio but he didn't. Where do them nigga's live, Big? I went over to the crib where Ricio used to stay and a whole other family lives there. The apartment Sosa used to live in has been vacant for six months. Max is the only one still living in the same spot because it belongs to you and his ass don't have to pay shit."

"I don't know about any of that. When I got locked up, I never thought to contact them about anything other than my money. Shit, yo' ass is out there with them, why you don't know?"

"When I see them it's always at the traps or they are at my crib. I don't fuck with their young asses like that, I'm a grown ass man. The only thing I'm worried about is if all the money accounted for. Anything else is not my concern."

"Floyd, I need you to find out where they are hiding out. I want my money from that muthafucka tonight! I gotta go because I hear them getting ready to count. Holla at me when

you hear something, hit me with a text and I'll call you back."
I said hanging up.

Mauricio was clever. He had to have been thinking about all this shit for some time because he definitely had his ducks in a row. Who moves out of their crib without giving anyone notice? Somebody that's got plans that he's ready to execute. He has to wake up early as hell to try to come for my shit, I wasn't giving nothing up without a fight. My crew was going to ride with me even if I was wrong, including Max.

I had been telling him a lot of shit that may have him looking at his brother's crazy. Letting him know that his brother thought he was soft and wasn't built for the streets. That pushed him out in the streets deeper than I anticipated but it paid off for me because he was one of my top workers. Max could handle a gun with the best of them and I made that happen by taking him to the gun range three times a week for the past four years. I taught him everything he needed to know about the streets and drugs.

Reese didn't want his sons to have anything to do with the drug game. They weren't my kids to raise but I didn't have a problem with grooming them into dope boys. That was the only way they were going to sleep under my roof, they had to work for their keep.

All three of them had money from the house, cars, and dope that their parents left behind. I didn't let them know about any of that shit. Reese owed me that money for all the years of work I'd put in. Besides, they couldn't trip over something they knew nothing about. As far as they knew, working for me was the only way to go.

I wasn't so sure about that now, Mauricio knew too much. There was no telling what else he had in his possession. Time would tell and all I could do was sit back until I got the call from Floyd. My cellie came back and went to the commode. This nigga waited all day to come in this muthafucka to shit.

"Yo ass better flush with every fuckin' turd too, nigga! Don't nobody want to smell that bullshit!" I bellowed out to his ass.

"I'm not trying to hear that shit! My stomach was boiling so I came in to release the shit. Come on man, let me take care of my business in peace!"

"Carter! Matthews! What the hell y'all hollering about tonight? You two should gone down to the chapel and get married. Y'all sound like an old married couple every damn day. Keep that shit down because I don't want to have to come back in here." Officer Thomas said in his southern drawl.

"You counted two niggas in this bitch, now get the fuck out." I gritted at his punk ass.

I couldn't stand his white ass. he always had something to say and he always said that shit like he had authority. I didn't give a fuck about him being a guard, I would beat his ass. I tried my best not to let the shit he said bother me, but I didn't know how long I would be able to hold off.

"Thomas, get the fuck out of my house! Why do we have to go through *this* shit every night? Get out!"

"I'm going, but I'll be back at eleven, boy." He said laughing.

"I ain't ya boy, bitch. When you come back you better count from the door and leave your pale ass right back out." I said turning over facing the wall.

My lawyer needed to hurry up and get me out of this muthafucka before I killed somebody in this prison. Thomas was going to be the first on my list, then I was going to cut Matthews intestines out because his ass smelled like something crawled in his ass and died.

MEESHA

Chapter 9
Sosa

Ricio stayed at my house talking about everything that Beast and my Pops told him. Reese muthafuckin' Williams was a genius. Only a man that wanted to protect his business and his family would have some shit in place before he died. When Ricio told me about the storage unit and all the drugs, I knew our days of working for Big Jim were over. We had enough product to throw around the city to make it look like it was snowing in July.

We made plans to go check out the unit tomorrow, along with going to the bank to see what was inside the deposit box. Ricio talked to Max, I hoped he listened and went to a hotel. If they came for anyone, it would be him because he was the weakest out of the three of us.

"I'm calling up our backup. I told you, we can't go alone."

"I'll send a mass text for them to get here now. I already know who you gon' hit up." I said pulling out my phone.

Butta, Psycho, AK, Face, Felon, Fats: Aye fam, drop what ya doing and get to my crib now!

I sent the text and before I could place my phone back on my hip, it started going off back to back. Each text responded with the same message, "say less." That's one thing I could say about those niggas, there was no questions asked, they just reacted. They were our brothers from other mothers and it's been that way since we were in grade school.

"Everybody should be here within thirty minutes, all of them responded." I said going to my closet and pushing the button to open the hidden door.

"Aight, bet. I'll explain what's going on when we head out. We are taking the bulletproof Navigator, just in case things go awry." Ricio said. In the next breath, he started talking again and I was confused. "I wanted to let you know, me and Sosa is about to go pay Floyd a visit. I'm gon' give him this money and then we're done with his ass."

"Who the hell are you talking to?" I asked walking out of the closet.

"I'm talking to Beast," he whispered.

I nodded my head and went back to the closet and chose a couple of guns for Ricio to choose from. Laying the tools on the counter, the doorbell sounded and I headed to the door. I looked through the peephole and saw all my A1's standing on the other side. I quickly opened the door, and stepped to the side to let them in.

"What's up, Sosa? Who we fuckin' up?" Psycho's voiced boomed through the foyer.

"Ricio found out some shit about my father's murder. Big Jim did it."

"Wait hold the fuck up! His ass been running around like he's been helping y'all and he's the one that knocked off Reese! Big Jim was his nigga, man! Why would he do that shit?" Butta chimed in.

"The nigga was jealous and wanted to be the muthafuckin' man!" Ricio said walking into the room. "We're going to see Floyd. That nigga got me out here lookin' like a thief because I haven't brought my take for the week to him. After I return the money, I'm done with Big Jim and his crew. Are y'all with us on this?" he asked looking around the room at the people that had been in his corner from diapers.

"Hell yeah, I'm standing ten toes down with y'all. I'm not working for a fuckin' snake! We'll find another way to make this money. All we have to do is put our money together and find a connect. We gon' take over their entire empire. It's gon' take a minute but we on that shit." Felon said.

The rest of them agreed and everybody started talking at once. "Hold on! All that sounds good. I want y'all to know that I don't need ya money. We are about to flood these streets with the purest cocaine from Columbia, the same kind my father had when he was the king of the streets." Ricio explained.

"We killin' them muthafuckas right?" AK asked with his arms folded over his chest.

"If it comes to that we will. Tonight, we're only going to give them their money back." I said walking to the counter where the guns were.

"Man, fuck that! I know y'all don't think these niggas ain't gon' be on bullshit. They won't accept that money then call a truce, Ricio. We got to lay them muthafuckas down, tonight! As a matter of fact, I say keep the money, fuck them!" Felon yelled pacing back and forth.

"Nah, Felon. I think Sosa is on to something. Floyd gon' expect us to come on some strong-arm shit. We won't make it easy for them to read us. As much as I want to agree about not returning the money, we have to give it back. Then we run through their shit and take all they shit! All of it belongs to the big homie, Reese. And we getting it back. But tonight, we about to look like a group of lame dope boys. But soon, we will be working hard as fuck to come up with a plan to take over this muthafuckin' city!" Butta growled.

Butta had a point with what he said and I was digging his logic. In my mind I knew he would be the brains of the organization. We were going to do exactly what he said and walk away from that shit like the bosses we were about to be.

"Y'all ready to roll out? I know you niggas came strapped, right?" I asked.

All six of them came up with their tools, "we stay ready, nigga! Don't insult a real one." Fats said.

"We rollin' in the Navigator tonight fellas, let me shoot this nigga Floyd a text." Ricio said pulling out his phone. He sent the text and we waited to see where we were headed. A few minutes later, Floyd replied. "He wants to meet on 26th, let's go."

"Hold up, I gotta go to my ride." AK said walking to the door.

"What you forget?" I asked him before he could leave out.

"Shid, I left the Choppa in that bitch. I can't roll without my namesake, nigga. Shit just wouldn't be right if she wasn't by my side. I may have to spray the whole block up, you never know." He said with a smirk.

"That nigga crazy. Who's stepping up to babysit his ass because he's gonna set shit off." Fats said laughing.

"I think he'll be okay, we are not going to start a body count, yet." Ricio said chuckling while placing the gun he chose in the holster he had on.

"You better explain that shit to that nigga because he don't take Precious along with him unless he's about to make her big ass clap."

"Now that's a muthafuckin' fact, nigga!" AK vouched as he walked back in with his bitch draped in a gun cover.

"AK, we are not killing anybody tonight, fam." I said laughing at his ass.

"Y'all don't know what the fuck gon' happen. This Chicago. Niggas get popped standing on their porch minding their own muthnafuckin' business! I'm that nigga that stay ready for whateva. I'm not givin' these pussies a chance to get me because I wasn't ready. Let's go!" he said walking to the garage where the Navigator was.

We all piled in the truck and all types of thoughts rolled through my head. I had a funny feeling in my stomach and I didn't like it. Fats was the driver and Ricio was in the passenger seat up front. The rest of us climbed in the back. We rolled on the expressway doing about seventy-five and it was quiet as hell in the truck.

"Damn nigga, happy birthday! I almost forgot." Psycho said to Ricio. "What a way to spend yo' muthafuckin' birthday."

"Yeah, I found out a lot of shit today and I can honestly say, this has been a very emotional birthday. I wouldn't change shit about today, it happened for a reason and I'm glad it did." Ricio said looking out the window.

"Shid on my birthday, I don't want no bullshit taking place, I will be deep in some pussy or getting my dick sucked. I'm puttin' my raincheck in now. Fuck that!" Face bust out and we all laughed.

"You a fool, nigga." Fats said as he pulled up on 26th Street. I stared out the window as we rolled down the block.

"What the fuck is his stupid ass doing out here? I told him to lay low!" Ricio's voice filled the truck.

I spotted Max standing laughing it up with Red. He was hardheaded as fuck. My blood was boiling because he didn't believe fat meat was greasy with his stupid ass. Fats pulled the truck into a park in front of the trap and we all jumped out. All smiles fell from their faces and Floyd stepped forward with Shake, John John, and Red behind him.

"It took you all day to bring my money, Ricio. I don't do thieves. When I call yo' ass from this point on, you answer. I shouldn't have to call repeatedly and still don't get you on the line."

"How the fuck did I steal yo' shit if I got it right here? That shit sound stupid as hell, Floyd." I sneered throwing the duffle bag at his feet. "One thing you should know about me is, I don't dance to nobody's drum but my own. You not talking to one of the niggas standing behind you, my name is Mauricio, nigga. You got yo' money and you don't have to worry 'bout me and my brothers no more. We quit. Come on, Max."

Floyd laughed as he turned around to look at Max. My brother didn't move an inch, he stood strong behind this nigga. "See, Ricio, Max belongs to Big Jim. He knows his place in this empire and he's hungry. Leaving with you only means he would starve, he wants to continue to eat. Money trumps blood all day in the drug business. I'm gon' give you a pass for disrespecting the Boss, because it's yo' birthday. Don't ever let that shit happen again!"

"Was that shit supposed to move me or something? Well it didn't! Max don't belong to nobody but Reese, nigga! Since he's not here, his ass belongs to me! Now let's go Max!"

Max stood there like he didn't know which way to go. It pissed me off because he shouldn't have to think about the shit at all. "What the fuck you waiting on? Get the fuck over here and let's go!" I barked while walking forward.

Max made his way through John John and Red to get to me. When he tried to pass Floyd, he grabbed Max's arm and got in his face. Max's eyes shifted from me to Floyd with fear in them. Floyd leaned over and whispered something in his ear and my brother's face showed he was scared of him. I reached out and snatched Max toward me and was face to face with Floyd.

"You want to repeat what you said to him?"

"I asked him was he ready to die nigga. That's the only way you muthafuckas getting out the crew. Ain't no muthafuckin' leaving because you don't want to be here no mo."

"Yo' ass is out ya mind, bitch! We out and that's the end of it. Who gon' make me stay, nigga?" I said pressing my nose against his.

Floyd pushed me back and I rocked his ass without hesitating. His head swung to the side and he raised up holding his jaw. "I see yo' young ass got heart. Yo' daddy had that same drive, look where that got him." he laughed. Like I said, I'm gon' give you a pass, but I'll be waiting for y'all to run this trap as usual."

"Wait on it, nigga, I'll see you around, punk."

I walked away from him as I grabbed Max by the arm and led him to the truck. Floyd thought he was one hard muthfucka but he wasn't shit without Big Jim. Once Max and I got in the truck I went in on ass his.

"Didn't Ricio tell you to lay low? What the fuck are you doing out here, Max?"

"Sosa, I need to get this money—"

"You want to make money with niggas that killed yo' father, muthafucka?" Before I could stop myself, I punched his ass in his jaw and kept beating the fuck out of him. "They killed Pop, and you still trying to eat with them niggas! I heard the shit with my own ears, they did that shit!" I screamed punching him once more. "Floyd just threw a subliminal about dad and yo' goofy ass didn't even catch it! You a lost cause, bro. They will kill you because you are Reese's son! They would kill you to hurt me and Ricio! Stay the fuck away from them!"

"Sosa, how the fuck am I supposed to eat? I need this money!"

"You don't' need shit! We got you! You gon' be straight, Max. Trust us."

"I'll give y'all a week. If I don't see no movement, I'm coming back." He had the nerve to say. Big Jim corrupted my little brother's mind and he thought his life revolved around selling drugs. He didn't understand the drug life goes beyond that.

"I can't tell you what to do, Max. We are just looking out for yo' stupid ass! But do what you want to do and don't say we didn't warn you." I said getting out of the truck.

Ricio was now standing in front of Shake and the words were getting vicious. "Nigga how the fuck you gon' say he killed Reese and you wasn't even there?" Shake screamed at Ricio.

"I know for a fact that nigga killed both of my parents, if he didn't, he knows who did. That's just like he pulled the trigga himself because he didn't forewarn him about it. You standing here defending a muthafucka harder than his nigga right here," I said pointing at Floyd. Don't let these bitches have you out here looking stupid. Floyd ain't saying shit because he knows what the fuck went down that night. Don't you fluky?" Ricio said with his nose flaring.

"Ricio, if you looking for a battle, you just started one. We ain't gon' ignore the disrespect yo' ass keep dishing out." Shake said venomously.

"This ain't *You Got Served,* nigga! I don't do battles, I go to war. There's a lot of room for all of us to eat out here. But since Reese had the whole muthafuckin' city on lock, I want what's rightfully mine. Get ready to move the fuck outta the way or get rolled the fuck over. The choice is yours. I'm done with this crew and I'm riding with the niggas that's riding with me, not against me. If death is the only way for me to get out, as you say, let's play the game of catch one, catch all, mufucka. I'm ready!" Ricio said turning his back.

Shake up his pistol and I had my nine in his face faster than lightening. Before he could blink there were seven guns aimed at his head. Ricio turned back around with a smirk on his face, "Don't pull ya gun if you don't plan on using it, hoe ass nigga. It's about to be on because the Renegade Boys about to ring bells all over this muthafucka. Tell yo' boss I said, get his weight up."

Ricio walked away and got in the truck. We still had our guns pointed at Shake's bitch ass just in case he wanted to be on some slick shit. Floyd reached over and pushed his arm down to lower his weapon. "Let's go," he said walking up the walkway to the trap.

"They about to be a huge problem, Sosa. We just gave them a chance to come at our heads. Max needs to stay the fuck away from those grimy niggas, real shit." Psycho said as we moved backwards to the truck.

MEESHA

Chapter 10
Nija

It was damn near midnight and I couldn't sleep to save my life. I hadn't heard from Ricio and I was worried. Beast said he wanted him to come over because he had something to talk to him about, but I hadn't heard from him since I left his house this morning. We'd spent the night watching movies before I drifted off to sleep. I got my best sleep when I was snuggled against his body.

Getting up out of the bed, I walked to the kitchen to get a glass of cranberry juice because my throat was dry. As I was opening the refrigerator, I heard my phone ringing in my bedroom. I raced to catch the call before the voicemail picked up.

"Hello," I said breathing hard into the phone.

"What the hell you over there doing, Nija?" Ricio's voice came through the speaker loudly.

"Nothing, and why are you yelling?"

"Yo' ass doing something because you all out of breath and shit."

"Ricio, I was in the kitchen when I heard my phone ringing. I had to run to get it. Why the fuck am I explaining anything to you anyway?"

I hated when his ass decided to get jealous and shit when he had a tribe of bitches running behind him. He was the one that was always talking about he didn't want to mess up our friendship. I couldn't understand that for anything in the world, but he wanted to question me about every aspect of my life.

"That's all you better been doing. I was calling to let you know I was down the street. Get ready to open the door." he said hanging up without giving me a chance to protest.

His birthday would be over by the time he got here. I would be cussing his black ass out as soon as he walked through the door. Throwing on a pair of boy shorts and a tank, I went back to the front of the house and stood in front of the window so I could see when he pulled up. After five minutes of waiting I decided to go get my juice out of the fridge.

I got halfway across the room and I heard a car door slam. An instant attitude took over my being. Mauricio was ringing the doorbell before I could get to the door. Peeking through the side window, I stood there for a few seconds before he started talking shit to me.

"Nija, open the fuckin' door man! I don't feel like going through this shit with you right now."

"Apologize first, Ricio."

"For what? I didn't do nothing wrong! Stop playing with me and open the door!"

"You hung up on me. That calls for an apology."

"I didn't hang up on you, there was nothing left to say Ni. Now, unlock the damn door, please."

The expression he wore told me something happened. Not to mention, he wasn't his happy go lucky self. I unlocked the door and pulled it open so he could come in. I closed and locked the door after he entered. My best friend looked worried and worn out. I wasn't about to try to figure out what was wrong, he'd open up and tell me eventually.

"Did you cook today? I haven't eaten since earlier and I'm starving", he said walking to the bathroom to wash his hands. While he took care of that, I headed to the kitchen to fix him a plate. I cooked fried catfish, spaghetti with ground turkey meat, cheese, garlic bread, and salad earlier. Placing a heaping portion of everything on a plate, I put it in the microwave to warm up. Once I put the Tupperware bowls back in the fridge, I heard Mauricio entering the kitchen.

"You didn't answer my question, did you cook?" he asked smacking me on my ass.

"Can't you smell the aroma of food in the air? Keep your hands to yourself please."

"What I tell you about that shit, Ni?"

"I don't know what you're referring to, Ricio."

"You know what the hell I'm talking about. Answering a question with a question."

The timer on the microwave sounded as I stood staring at him like he was stupid. He pushed the button to open it and stuck his finger in the middle of the spaghetti. It couldn't have been warm enough because he closed the door and set the timer again.

"We never had a conversation about that, Ricio. You've got your females mixed up, boo" I said rolling my eyes.

"I don't ever mix you up with nobody. Get yo' ass out of here talking that bullshit." He said taking his food out of the microwave.

"Well tell me where it came from then. You were adamant about it so, I know it's been discussed somewhere. You know what? Don't even worry about it, enjoy your food. I'll be in my room and no you can't eat in there." I said walking out of the kitchen.

"Ni, you ain't gon' keep me company?" he yelled behind me.

Ignoring his ass, I continued down the hall. Entering my room, I sat on the foot of the bed and checked myself. "You need to get ya feelings together, Nija. Things are not what you wish they were. Stop thinking about what he has going on in his life." I said to myself.

I didn't know how long I had been sitting there because I was reminiscing about all the things I had been through with Mauricio. Thinking back on it, we've been through many ups and downs together. There was nothing that could break the bond we had. As for taking what we have to the next level, he would have to be all about me. Starting with, releasing all his little hoes from under his nut sack. Until then, we will be just that, friends.

"What are you thinking about?"

Snapping out of my daze, I glanced up and he was leaned against the doorframe staring at me. He was looking too good at damn near one in the morning. It should be against the law for him to be so fine.

His deep brown eyes were trained on me like daggers. The way his shirt was hugging the muscles in his chest was changing the way I breathed. I glanced down at his legs and felt a tingle down my spine.

"Nija, what's on your mind?" he asked again.

"Nothing much. Did you enjoy your birthday?" I said changing the subject about my thoughts.

"So much happened today, Ni. I don't even know where to start." he sighed.

"Come talk to me and start from the beginning." I said patting the bed next to me.

He strolled slowly across the room and sat beside me. Quietly he wrapped me in his arms and buried his head in the crook of my neck. I automatically hugged him close as I felt his body tremble against me. Mauricio had been putting up a front about how bad he was hurting for years, this was the first time he'd let it out.

"It's about time you are letting this shit out. You've been holding it in for so long." I said rubbing his back. "It's gonna be okay, Ricio."

"Those niggas killed him, Ni!" He cried squeezing me tightly. "They killed him."

I didn't know who 'they' were, but I needed him to tell me what was going on. He released me after about five minutes and ran his hand down his face to dry the tears that continued to fall. In a blink of an eye, the sorrow turned into anger.

"Big Jim set Papí up, Ni. That mufucka wanted to be him so bad that he had him killed!"

"That's what Beast wanted to talk to you about?" I was shocked to hear him say Big Jim was the reason his dad wasn't with him anymore. They were always together and there never appeared to be any animosity between them.

"Nah, Beast wanted me to hear first-hand what Papí wanted to tell me. I heard the words directly from him. Everything he said was true because Reese Williams didn't lie about shit! He didn't have reasons to. I went to pay that nigga a visit today." He stopped talking after that statement.

"Who did you visit? Big Jim?"

"Hell yeah, I did! I had to get answers. He was trying to lie at first but his ass realized I knew too much for him to lie his way out of it. I let him know that I was coming for what is rightfully mine. They fucked up letting me find out about this shit! Papí didn't deserve to die behind a greedy muthafucka! All of them niggas gon' get handled! I already told Floyd what it is."

"Ricio, I think you need to calm down and think about this before—"

"Ain't shit to think about! All I'm about to do is strategize on how I'm about to break these niggas pockets, take back what belongs to me, and lead their ass to the highway to heaven so Reese can kill their asses again! I also have to figure out how I'm gon' keep Max's dumb ass away from them. He is not using his fuckin' head, man. He's not understanding, they will use him as bait. I told his ass to lay low and when I pulled up to holla at Floyd, his ass was standing amongst these niggas. If I have to keep beating his ass until he gets what the fuck I'm telling him, then that's what it's gon' be."

"I will talk to Max. Constantly putting your hands on him is going to make him cling to them more, Ricio. Y'all are like my family, I hate this is happening but I need you to have a level head. Don't jump out there on some gung-ho shit without thinking things through, okay?"

"I hear what you're saying but you would be wasting your breath trying to talk to Max. I don't know what kind of hold they've got on him, but I need him to know that his side to be on is over here. Big Jim don't give a fuck about him! If he did, he wouldn't have him out in these streets. Max should be in school trying to be better than this street shit."

"I agree and I will handle Max. Tell me how you heard these things from Reese." I said scooting back on the bed a bit.

Staring at the floor, Ricio was silent. When he lifted his head and looked at me, he smiled. "I heard his voice for the first time in four years, Ni. It was like he was there in the flesh. The shit felt so real. There is a disk telling us all his suspicions about Big Jim. He had everything in place if anything should happen to him. He told it all. I won't go into detail about what was said because I don't want to put you in harm's way. The less you know the better. What I will say is this, I got you Ni."

I didn't know what he was talking about and I didn't question him further. He talked about his parents for an hour straight and I sat and listened. This was the first time he talked about them without forcing himself to stop. I was glad because he needed to express the way he was feeling.

"I want to go to their gravesite later. Will you be able to call off to go with me? I'll give you the money that you will be missing out on for the day."

"I would be glad to go with you for support. You know I've been here since the day we met. Let me send an email to my boss and let her know I won't be in. There is no need for you to pay me for being there for you, that's what paid time off is for." I said with a smile.

After sending the email I crawled to the head of the bed and snuggled under the covers. Ricio had revealed a lot of things and it drained me just listening. He was sitting quietly staring straight ahead. His shoulders were slumped and he looked defeated from the angle I was seeing him.

"Ricio, come lay down and relax. Take your mind of the events of today, if only for a couple hours." I said softly.

"Nothing but revenge can take my mind off what I found out today, Ni. I don't even feel like myself. To be honest, I haven't felt like myself in years. I'm not the same Mauricio Vasquez from four years ago. Shit, the nigga I was yesterday is gone, he has been replaced too. I need you to pray that I come back from the shit that I plan to do. Only a nigga with no heart would be thinking of the things that's running through my mind."

I pushed myself up and crawled to him and wrapped my arms around his neck. "Everything will be okay, you need to rest." I said moving my hand up and down his back.

"Sleep will not come when I have so much on my mind. My body is bone tired but my mind is running a marathon. There's so much shit that's coming at me full force all at once."

I knew what it was like to have your brain on overload but I had no clue what he was going through in this situation. All I knew was he needed to rest before he worried himself to death. Lifting the hem of his shirt, I pulled it up his stomach and over his head. Forcing him to raise his arms. I threw his shirt in the chair by the window, got out of bed and stood in front of him. Taking his hands in mine, I motioned for him to stand.

He stood slowly and I unbuckled his belt, then unbuttoned his pants. As I pulled them down along with his boxers, he grabbed my hand. I glanced up at him and his arms fell to his side. When his pants hit the floor, I fell to my knees and inserted his semi erect penis into my mouth. I took a couple deep breaths through my nose because even though he didn't have a full erection, Ricio was hung like a horse. Closing my eyes, I raised my hand and wrapped it around his thick pole and swallowed all nine inches.

"Ssssss, if you gon' do that shit, Ni. Do it right. You already know we don't do hands. Let me see what that mouth do, ma."

I lowered my hands and he pumped his hips slowly and I caught on to the rhythm instantly. Relaxing my throat, I suctioned hard and allowed the tip to hit my tonsils with every stroke. He grabbed my hair with both hands and lifted up on his toes while going deeper.

"Shit, Ni! Suck that shit just like that! Damn!"

I cradled his balls in my hand, massaging them gently as I moved them forward. Gliding the tip of my tongue along them, I used my finger to caress the spot between his balls and his asshole and he paused for a second. His legs gave way and he fell back on the bed. I moved right along with him without breaking contact with his dick.

"Ni, What the fuck! Oooouu shit, girl!" he groaned when I found the spot a second time.

His back lowered to the bed and I let the saliva build up in my mouth so I could get porn star nasty with the dick. Easing his pole from my mouth, I started stroking him slowly as I replaced my finger with my tongue. I put pressure on the spot and as I continued to stroke him, his body tensed up. I could feel him swell more in my hand and I knew he was about to release all of his babies.

"Shit, that feels good. Nija, I'm about to cum baby!"

I focused on that spot and his groans became louder. My pussy was wet and my clit was aching with every sound he made. Placing my hand between my legs I massaged my bud ferociously because I wanted us to get that nut together. I was pleasing both of us at the same damn time and I was enjoying every bit of it. I stroked him faster and rubbed myself at the same pace. A moan escaped my throat and the vibration sent him over the edge.

"Nija! Fuck!" he screamed out as I felt the warm liquid flowing between my fingers with every stroke. "Aaaah, yeah!" he said breathing hard. "That's enough! That's enough!" he said pushing my head away from him.

Sitting on my knees I smirked as he tried to catch his breath. His python still had cum leaking from it, my mouth salivated as I stared. Leaning forward, I ran my tongued along the head and wrapped my lips around it and sucked it up. *"There was no need for that good protein to go to waste."* I thought to myself.

"Nijaaaaaa!"

His pole was coming back to life but he pushed my head back and grilled my ass. I couldn't do anything but laugh because he hated when I one upped him. He was one of those men that had to be in control at all times in the bedroom.

"Yo' ass plays too much, Ni. I'm gon' show you better than I can tell you though. Got me in this mufucka sounding like a bitch! Nah, I can't have that shit." He said standing up.

"I didn't do nothing," I said laughing harder.

"Oh, you think it's funny, huh?" he said stroking his dick. "Payback is a mufucka but you gon' love what I got in store for you."

"Ricio, I'm sleepy. I just wanted you to relax and it worked." I said with a smirk.

"It definitely did that, but let me show you what else it did." he said scooping me up in his arms.

Ricio placed me on top of the dresser and spread my legs wide. He stared at my clean shaved pussy while licking his lips. As he ran his hands up and down my thighs, his thumb rubbed against my nub. The electric current traveled up my spine and I moaned softly. He got on his knees and pulled me forward until my ass was hanging off the edge.

"Spread yo' mufuckin' legs and you bet not close 'em." He demanded as I did what he instructed.

When his mouth covered my kitty, I lost all my senses. I couldn't see, hear, taste the spit in my mouth, smell, nor touch anything. He was devouring my love box like he hadn't just finish eating an hour ago. My head fell back against the dresser and my breathing became erratic. The moans that escaped my mouth sounded like hiccups because I couldn't catch my breath. I tried to move away from his mouth but he snatched me back with his strong arms. I closed my legs and he looked up at me without stopping and pried them back open.

"Oh shit!" I moaned when he stuck his tongue deep into my tunnel and fucked me with it.

My stomach muscles tightened and I knew I was about to explode. Trying my best to hold off, I was losing the battle with every curl of his tongue. He clamped down hard on my bud and the well broke.

"Yassssssss, I screamed as I squirted long and hard into his mouth.

He released my clit and sat back with his mouth open to catch every drop. Ricio stood to his feet and rubbed his pole up and down my slit. Tapping the head hard against it, I started squirting again. My hands clutched the dresser because it felt like I was floating in the air. Before I could get my mind right, I felt him enter me slowly.

Lifting my legs over his arms and pulling my ass completely off the dresser, he pounded me with long hard strokes. It felt so good that I was pulling my own damn hair. My titties were bouncing around until one popped out the top of my tank. He took that opportunity to grasp my nipple between his lips and suckled hard.

"Ricio damn, what are you doing to me? Ooooouuuuu!"

"I told yo' ass I was gon' pay you back. I want you to feel the same way you had me feeling a moment ago. The only difference is, you won't be able to make me stop. I'm gon' be in this tight pussy until I say when."

He placed his thumb on my clit and rubbed it vigorously. I was losing my damn mind and couldn't do anything but take it. The way he was fucking me was different. I couldn't wrap my head around the change, but I knew I felt the difference.

My eyes eased closed, "nope, open yo' fuckin' eyes and look at me while I'm making you feel good, Ni. This my pussy, right?"

Snapping my eyes open, I couldn't find my voice to answer him. "This my pussy, Ni?" he repeated. I shook my head up and down because I couldn't say anything. "Let me hear you say this my pussy."

When I didn't say it, he started fucking me harder. It hurt so good and I welcomed the beating he was putting on my kitty. He went in deeper and it felt like the tip was going to come out through my mouth. I used my hand to push him back a bit, but he slapped it back down.

"Don't touch me, I'm running this shit now. You had your chance to put on a show, keep ya' hands to ya'self. This is my last time asking, is this my pussy, Nija?"

"No, it's mine." I said breathily.

"Wrong answer," he said and hit me with death strokes. Cupping my ass in both of his hands, he lifted me off the dresser and held me midair while he pounded in and out of my honey pot rapidly.

I couldn't do anything except lean back with my head hanging toward the floor. The blood rushed to my head and the tightness of my stomach caused me to cum hard. It didn't stop him from continuing to beat my kitty up because he had a point to prove.

"This my pussy, Ni. You don't have to admit the shit because I'm molding her ass to only respond to my dick." he said moving to the bed as he sat down. "Ride this mufucka like your life depends on it. You wanted me to relax, now's your chance to make it happen."

I was drained and I couldn't move to do what he wanted. He started pumping his hips up and down while holding my legs in the crook of his arms. My love box was open for all his dick to have access to and that shit was incredible. Wrapping my arms around his neck, I stuck my tongue in his mouth to suppress my moans but he pulled away. A moan flowed out loudly and I felt his dick get harder than what it already was.

"Aaaah yeah, this is the best pussy I've ever had. I love you, Ni." He said letting my legs down.

I placed my feet on the floor and moved sensually on his pipe. Caressing the back of his head, I rode the tip before I plopped on it repeatedly as I felt his nails digging into my ass cheeks. I felt his member pulsating and I knew he was on the brink of cumin'. Popping my pussy on the tip, I knew this was going to make him pop his top. I listened to his breathing speed up and I was ready to hop up before he came. My plan didn't work because he held me tightly as he released all his babies deep in my womb.

He fell back onto the bed and I laid my head on his chest. We both went to sleep in the position we landed in. Relaxation fell upon the both of us and it felt damn good.

MEESHA

Chapter 11
Maximo

My brothers are looking at me like I'm a fuckin' disappointment. They don't know why I have to stay on Big Jim's good side. Both Mauricio and Sosa are going to look at me differently and have a million and three questions that I may not even have the answers to. This shit went down on my bro's birthday and I didn't even salute him on his day.

Floyd talked all night about how he was going to kill my brothers. I wasn't going to sit back and let that shit happen. I tried telling him to just let them out but he wasn't trying to hear me. Floyd felt that both of them disrespected him in the streets and that was an automatic violation of the codes Big Jim put in place.

The only way for me to put a halt to this war that was brewing, I was going to have to go see Big Jim. I hadn't been to the prison to see him since he got locked up, but he called all the time. I only talked to him when I felt like doing so. The sound of his voice made my skin crawl. I didn't have any love for Big Jim, I was stuck between a rock and a hard place.

It was true he had been there for us and put money in our pockets, but he was far from the man he portrayed himself to be. I put on the front of being against my brothers so they would leave me alone to do what I had to in order to still be on the inside of the crew. When Ricio said they had something to do with the death of my father, I knew it could be true.

Big Jim was an evil man that would do whatever it took to get back at anyone he thought did him wrong. I just didn't know why he did the things he had done to me. I had never disrespected him in any way. He showed love for me in the streets, but hated me behind closed doors. He had me spooked and I couldn't say anything about it.

I woke up and went to the bathroom to drain my pipe. I was tired as fuck because I didn't sleep a wink after what happened last night. I knew that bullets were about to fly, but both sides held their anger in. How they did it was still a mystery to me. it wasn't over by a long shot, though. This was just the beginning and I knew how dirty Floyd and Big Jim could get.

After washing my hands, I went back into my bedroom and picked up my phone. Going to the contact I was looking for, I pressed the call button and sat on the edge of the bed. When the call connected, I stayed quiet until the person on the other end spoke.

"What the fuck you want so early in the morning, Max?" Beast's voice bellowed through the phone.

"I need you to get me in the prison to see Big Jim." I said with my head resting in my hand. "I have to stop this war that Mauricio started. Plus, I need to holla at him about something."

"Why the fuck you didn't go to Floyd's pussy ass to get you in to see yo' boss? That's the side you chose, right? Don't think I forgot I owe you an ass whoopin' lil nigga. The punks you give yo' loyalty may accept disrespect but you know I ain't going for that shit."

"Beast, I apologize for the shit I said and did. I was pissed because of the way Ricio came at me. When you called, I was pissed off and took it out on you."

"What the fuck did you expect him to do, Max? You upped a banga on yo' own muthafuckin' brother! You lucky he didn't lay yo' ass down. Family or not, I would've blown yo' head off. What the fuck you need to talk to this nigga about? I already know it ain't about the so-called war because that still stands regardless. They violated, ain't no getting out of that."

"I can't talk about it right now. Can you please get me a visit, please?"

"Y'all are on his list, he just don't know it. There's no specific day that you have to wait to see that bitch nigga. If you want to go today, you can. But let me make a call so they will be expecting you. One of these days, you will explain what the fuck his ass is dangling over your head, Max. Hit me up when you leave that muthafucka. From this day forth, I want to know your every fuckin' move. Is that understood?"

"Yeah, Beast. I got it. Thanks, I'll talk to you in a couple hours."

"Aight," he said hanging up.

I sat on the bed and thought about all the shit I had been through for the past couple years. Mauricio and Sosa left me and went to school and my life ain't been the same since. I died when my parents were killed and nobody knew what the fuck I'd been going through. With Floyd threatening to kill what was left of my family, I had to talk to Big Jim to put a stop to the bullshit.

Raising up from the bed, I went to the closet and grabbed a black and white Nike sweat suit. I wasn't trying to get all dressed up to go to the prison. As I headed to the bathroom to hop in the shower, my phone started ringing. I walked over to the other side of the room and picked it up and slid the button to the right.

"Yeah," I said into the phone.

"Everything is a go, remember what I said. Max." Beast said before hanging up.

I took a quick shower, dressed, and grabbed my keys, and wallet jetting out the crib. As I was hopping in my car, Floyd was pulling into the driveway. I didn't have time to fuck around with him, I had somewhere to be and he was not about to stand in the way of it. Opening the driver's door, I got in and shut the door while I inserted the key.

Floyd got out of the car and I backed up without looking at him. My phone started ringing and I glanced down at the screen. It was him calling but I didn't even attempt to answer the call. The phone kept ringing back to back like it was a bitch trying to find out where I was. Fuck Floyd, this shit was about to be over as soon as I talked to Big Jim.

The text chime filled the car and I reached over and turned the radio up loud. I found the rap station on Sirus radio and let the music entertain me for the entire two hours I was driving. My thoughts were making me angrier by the minute and I couldn't wait to get my chance to confront Big Jim.

My mind wandered back to the day of my father's funeral. It was as if I was having an out of body experience because I could hear the organ playing, the choir singing, and my mother's loud wails. I looked on as me and my brothers tried to console my mother the best that we knew how and it was breaking my heart all over again.

Taking my eyes off my mom, they landed on the black casket that sat in the front of the church. I still couldn't believe my father was laying in there cold as ice and I wouldn't see him again after that day. Feeling my eyes water, I tried to think about something besides the funeral, but I couldn't.

At that moment, I saw a young me running out of the sanctuary toward the restrooms. Mauricio started walking up the aisle to follow me and Big Jim stopped him. He nodded his head as Big Jim patted him on his shoulder and went back to my mother's side. Big Jim went in the direction I had gone and found me laid out on the floor, crying my eyes out.

As I watched Big Jim console me, I was seeing firsthand how he touched me inappropriately the very first time. He disrespected my father on the day of his funeral, in the church where his body laid in a casket. Forcing me to stroke his dick, then rubbed it against my lips. The only reason he didn't go further was because someone was coming toward the bathroom. Big Jim went into the stall to fix his clothes as if nothing was going on. He then led me back into the church and sat me beside him while he played in the back of my pants. Big Jim threatened to kill my whole family if I told anyone about what happened that day. That was when my life became a nightmare.

A car horn brought me back to the present and I almost ran into the back of a semi-truck. Swerving to avoid a collision, God was on my side because there wasn't another car in the next lane. I pulled over on the shoulder of the road and sat for a few moments. I needed to clear my mind before I killed myself. Looking at the GPS, I still had forty-five minutes to go before I would arrive at the prison.

Thoughts about the things I wanted to say to Big Jim overpowered my mind while I sat on the side of the highway. If he didn't agree to call off the war against my brothers, I'd have to give him an ultimatum of my own. But what if he doesn't accept? What would I do then? He would probably get mad and want to kill me too. I didn't give a fuck at that point. It had been long overdue and I didn't have a choice at that point. Fuck getting ready, I needed to *be* ready. Thinking to myself, *"there was nothing he could do to me with a guard close by."* Everything would have to be put on the table and I'd go from there. Pulling back onto the highway, I gave the road my full attention as I followed the directions to my destination.

When I pulled up in the parking lot of the prison, my mind screamed at me to back out and drive away. The fear for the man that I was going in to see came out full force. I tried calming myself but it wasn't working. My hands started shaking hard and my breathing quickened. I was having a hard time catching my breath and I'd never had any problems like that before. I was more afraid of what would happen to my brothers once I said what I knew I'd have to say to Big Jim.

The walk to the door felt like forever. I went to the counter and gave the woman behind the counter all the information she asked for. After she gave my ID back, I was instructed to sit until someone came out to escort me to the back. The guard called my name and I rose from the chair and walked where he was standing. He barely searched me before he led me to a small room that looked like an interrogation room.

"Carter will be brought out shortly. Would you like anything to drink while you wait?" he asked.

"Nah, I'm good." I said sitting back in the chair.

"Tell Beast, Chuck said what's up when you talk to him." he said leaving out closing the door behind him.

"Damn, Beast's reach is long as fuck." I thought to myself. I'd been sitting in the room for maybe thirty minutes before I heard movement outside the door.

"Who the fuck is here to see me on a muthafuckin' Wednesday, Chuck?"

"Man, I was told to bring yo' ass down here. That's all the fuck I know. I'll be right outside the door, all you got to do is tell me when you're ready to end the visit." Chuck said opening the door.

Big Jim entered the room with his hands cuffed in front of him. I glanced up and the scowl that he had on his face turned into a smile. My stomach started churning and I instantly felt the bile trying to come up. I closed my eyes and the images behind them had me shaking my head trying to erase every last one of them, it didn't work.

"What's up, Maxie?" he said with a chuckle as he sat down in the chair across from me.

"Don't call me that, Big Jim. I was named Maximo, not Maxie. Stop calling me that shit!"

"You didn't seem to mind when I was on the outside. What's the difference now?" he asked cockily.

"The difference is, you can't act on your sadistic ways in here. I need you to call off Floyd and the rest of the crew. They are talking about killing my brothers and I won't sit back and let that happen.

He laughed long and heartily while clutching his stomach. "What the fuck you mean you won't let it happen? Nigga, you ain't got no muthafuckin' say so in the matter! You got the game fucked up! Yo' brother disrespected me after everything I've done for y'all, then he tried to steal my money—"

"Big Jim, Mauricio wasn't stealing from you—"

"If yo' punk ass ever interrupts me when I'm talking again, I will kill you, bitch!" he snapped. "Ricio needs to be taught a fuckin' lesson and he is going to get it. I don't know what the fuck you thought coming here was gon' do. I'm not calling off shit! His ass is good as dead, nigga."

"Please, man! Don't do this shit. I don't have anybody left but them, I've already lost my parents, I can't lose them too." I was on the verge of tears because he wasn't willing to even consider what I was asking him.

"What the fuck are you going to do for me to save your brothers?" he asked while smirking at me. "I haven't felt yo' lips on my dick in a while. Give me that satisfaction right now, and I'll call that shit off today."

"I'm not doing none of that shit willingly! I didn't enjoy none of what you made me do for years! Why the hell did you do me like that, Big Jim? I need to know! The things you did to me got me out here fucking bitches left and right trying to figure out if I'm actually gay! You molested me, nigga! With a fucking gun to my head every time! Now you want to sit up here and act like I was your boy toy on purpose!"

"I did that shit because your daddy was a bitch ass nigga! You were paying for him treating me like a low budget street nigga. I got at his ass when I had his muthafuckin' head blown off and took over his shit. I chose you to take this dick up the ass because I'm still pissed at him. Since I couldn't bring him back to life and kill his ass again, I opted to fuck his weak ass son and get away with it. You will continue to do what the fuck I say and you better not tell a soul what the fuck I had you doing. Am I clear?"

Hearing him admit he had my father killed, did something to me. The anger that built up inside me was ready to come out. I knew I couldn't do anything to him in the prison, but I was ready to tarnish his name in the streets.

"Nah, you not clear. You won't stop what the fuck is planned for my brothers, that means I have to ruin yo' ass in return. Everything that you did to me will be known on the streets. I don't give a damn what people think happened, or if they think I'm gay. The truth will be told. Don't think I don't know that yo' ass is a down low nigga because I do. There were plenty of nights I heard you and that nigga Floyd moaning passionately in each other's ears. You had a whole nigga but you wanted to fuck with me!"

"Somebody is mad now, huh? I'm gon' tell you this, Maxie. If you think you are going to put my business in the street without any repercussions, think again. You are a dead man walking right along with yo' brothers. Don't go back to my house, you no longer live there. I hope you saved up some money because yo' dealing days are over with me. You can starve to death and I wouldn't give a fuck. The first person that says that Big Jim is a homo, your head is going to be delivered to your muthafuckin' brothers in a cardboard box.

138

Don't ever bring yo' ass back around me, nigga! Chuck let me out of here before I kill this punk!" he said standing up.

Big Jim had the look of death in his eyes as he stared at me. For the first time in years, I wasn't scared of him. He wanted to play tough, then I was ready to do what I had to do to blow up his spot. Fuck him and Floyd, I wasn't taking shit off them no more.

MEESHA

Chapter 12
Sosa

I was up putting the finishing touches on Ricio's surprise party. Truthfully speaking, I wanted to cancel this shit altogether because I knew that nigga Floyd had something up his sleeve after I rocked his punk ass. But Reese didn't raise no bitch niggas, we would have to be ready whenever them niggas came for us. I was ready to light the city up and make it look like the Fourth of July.

Max was making my ass itch with his soft ass. I was going to need him to listen to what the fuck we were saying to him. He knows something because he has been acting differently for a while now, I just couldn't figure the shit out. He would have to open up. That would be the only way we could help him. If we didn't know what was going on, he would continue to deal with whatever it was on his own.

My phone started ringing next to my laptop, I glanced at it and it was Max. I snatched it up and answered it. "Max, what's up, brah?"

"Sosa, I need to lay my head at yo' spot for a minute. I'll explain everything when I get to you in a couple hours."

"What the fuck happened, Max?"

"Brah, would you just take my word, I will explain shit when I get back to the city!" he yelled into the phone before hanging up.

I didn't know what the fuck he had going on but I couldn't wait for him to pull up. I was about to call Ricio when my phone started ringing again. He must've been reading my mind because he was calling. I didn't hesitate to answer, I connected the call quick as fuck.

"Ricio, what's up?" I asked quickly.

"Shit, I was calling to make sure you were straight. What's going on, you sound nervous. Everything good?"

"I don't know. Max just called saying that he needed to crash at my spot for a minute but he didn't go into detail. I'm worried about him, Ricio. Whatever is going on with him didn't just come about last night, it has to be deeper than that. He will be by here when he gets back to the city."

"Where the fuck is he?"

"That's the thing, I don't know. Before I could ask, he banged on me."

"Aight, I'll be through there when I leave the cemetery. I had to come see mama and papí. We will find out what the fuck is going on when he touchdown."

"Aye, have you talked to Nija? I need to talk to her about something."

"What the hell you need to holla at her about?" he asked with suspicion.

"If you don't sit yo' jealous ass down somewhere, nigga. Answer the damn question." I chuckled.

"Hee hee my ass, muthafucka. Whatever you got to say to her, you can say to me."

"Nah, not this time brah. I'll call her myself."

"Oh no you won't! She's right here, hold on," he said. I heard low murmuring for a few seconds before Nija spoke softly into the phone.

"Hey, Sosa. What's going on?"

"Is his nosy ass looking in your mouth?"

"You know it." she said laughing.

"Okay, well just listen. I was going to cancel the party because we got some shit going on right now, but I decided not to. Have you had the chance to figure out how you were going to get him to the strip club? Yes or no."

"No, not yet. But I will."

142

"Alright. Remember it's an all-white event, we're about to bring his twenty-first in with a bang! We have two days before the party, I'm wrapping shit up and everything will be set to go."

"Okay, cool. Thanks, brah."

"That's my bro and I have to get his mind off things for a bit, let him enjoy his day. He deserves it."

"Let me go, this fool should be able to tell me what my tonsils look like the way he is all in my shit." She said laughing.

"Both of you muthafuckas gon' get beat the fuck up, stop playing with me! Give me my damn phone."

Nija could be heard laughing in the background, while Ricio was breathing hard into the phone. "Brah, let me find out y'all creeping around. I'll forget that I'm my brother's keeper over that one."

"Stop playing with her and lock her down, nigga. You wouldn't have to worry about lil shit like that. But for real though, this ain't that. Get ya panties outta bunch, punk."

"What is it then?" he asked.

"None of yo' muthafuckin' business. Get here, nigga!" I said hanging up.

Ricio was something else. He needed to tell that girl how the fuck he felt about her and claim her. Instead of getting jealous about every damn thing she does. All those other cum banks don't mean shit to him, I didn't understand what the fuck he was doing with his sex life. Hopefully he will get it together soon.

My mind drifted back to Max and I needed to talk to somebody about him. I decided to hit Beast up to see if he knew anything. As I was scrolling through my phone, it started ringing. When I saw Jess' name pop up I got mad instantly because I told her bird brain ass I was done with her. The shit she pulled had me wanting to go back to her crib and kick her ass. I let it go to voicemail but she called right back.

"Didn't I tell yo' thieving ass to lose my number, bitch?" I asked after answering without saying hello.

"Sosa, I'm sorry. I want to give you the money I took back. I'd rather have you than seven hundred dollars."

"Oh no, bitch! You made your choice when you searched through my shit without permission. I'm good on that. Keep that shit and don't contact me no mo'. If I have to tell yo' ass again, I'm fuckin' you up! I don't need a bitch by my side that I can't trust, you fucked that up on ya own. Now get the fuck off my line!"

I hung up on her ass and went back to scrolling through my phone. When I got to Beast's number, a text came through. "This bitch think I'm playing with her hoe ass." I said out loud. I didn't even read the message, instead I pressed the phone icon and called Beast.

"Nephew, what it do?" he ask.

"Chillin'. I wanted to ask you something. Have you talked to Max?"

"Yeah, I talked to him this morning. Everything good?"

"I'on no. He called and said he needed to crash at my place for a minute, but he didn't say much else. He said he would fill me in when he got back to the city. Where did he say he was headed today?"

"He went to see Big Jim. He said he was going to try to stop the war between y'all and Floyd. Shit couldn't have gone well. I tried to tell him that he was wasting his time trying to talk to that nigga."

"Why the fuck would he go talk to Big Jim if he didn't even sit his ass down to listen to what all of this shit stemmed from. This is what I mean when I say his ass needs to listen!"

"Sosa, I'm gon' be real with you. I think it's deeper than Max is letting on. Something else has happened or he know something that nobody else knows. If he went to the prison to stop this war, he threw something at Big Jim to make him call it. I can tell you this, it didn't go as planned if yo' brother need a place to stay. I'm getting myself together and I'll be on my way."

"Beast, me and Ricio will handle this. If we need you, I'll call you myself. But what I do need you to do is, come through for Ricio's surprise birthday party that I'm giving him on Friday. It will be at Paradise Kitty. I need all the reinforcement I can get in case those niggas come for us."

"Nothing else needs to be explained. I will be there, but I won't be there. You know how I roll. When you see Sin, you will know I'm in the building."

"Bet. The doors open at ten. I know you won't be there at ten, but I need you to be there."

"Nah, with these niggas lurking about, I'll be there before yo' ass do. I will have to be in place to keep my eyes on shit while you boys have a good time. I suggest y'all let everybody else get fucked up. Y'all need to keep ya minds right and yo' eyes open at all times."

"Thanks Beast."

"You don't need to thank me. I'm here to look after y'all and that's what I will do. I didn't do a good job with Reese, but I'd be damned if these muthafuckas bring y'all down under my nose. They want beef, they got it. First thing Monday, we will start getting this empire together."

"Fo sho! I'm ready, for this shit."

"Aight, nephew. I have to get off this phone before Sin starts talking crazy. You know how she is when she's not getting my undivided attention."

"Bet. I'll holla atcha later."

Beast hung up and I chuckled while going back to my laptop to check the event page I made on social media. There were many people saying they were coming out to help celebrate my brother's birthday. This party was about to be lit. I just hoped we could party with no problems.

***

I finished my business with the party and laid back on my couch watching the baseball game. The Chicago Cubs were playing the St. Louis Cardinals on the road to clinch the division. The boys in blue were tearing a lining out of their ass, ten to four in the eighth. It still stands, their pitching sucked.

Not realizing I had dosed off, I heard my alarm beep indicating a muthafucka was coming in my shit. I reached under the cushion grabbing my nine-millimeter Sig Sauer and sat up. It sounded like someone was creeping along the foyer, but it didn't matter because I was ready. When the figure emerged in the family room where I was, there was a red beam front and center.

"What the fuck is yo' problem, Sosa? Get that shit out my face!" Ricio barked while pushing Nija behind him.

"I don't have a problem, brah. With the shit Big Jim and Floyd is on, I'm ready for whatever. Yo' ass need to let a nigga know when you are coming in. Holla my name, say aye, something so I won't have to lock and load on ya ass."

"Crazy muthafucka. Fuck them niggas, they ain't on shit. Have you heard from Max?" he asked.

"Nah, he hasn't called, let me call him to see where he is." I said reaching for my phone.

I dialed him up and waited for him to pick up but the voicemail picked up. My nerves started twitching and I didn't want to jump to any conclusions so, I tried again. The phone rang a couple times and he picked up. I was relieved and let the breath out that I was holding.

"Where ya at, lil bro."

"I just made it back to the city. I'll be there as soon as I go to the house and get my shit."

"Uh uh, bring yo' ass straight to my crib. Don't go over there by yourself, Max. Are you fuckin' crazy?"

"Put that shit on speaker, Sosa." Ricio said sitting on the couch. I did what he asked and sat the phone on the coffee table.

"Max, listen to me and listen to me good. For the past couple days, we have been bumping heads, I need that shit to stop right now. Floyd and his cronies are not to be taken lightly. Whatever the fuck you got at that house, we will go out and buy again. Wherever you are, stop and come here, bro. We got you. I don't know what's going on, but obviously Sosa does. Are you hearing me?" Ricio asked.

"I just jumped on the expressway, Ricio. I'm on my way."

"Max don't go against me bro, bring yo' ass!'"

"Damn, I'm not. I told you I was on my way. I'll be there in twenty." He said hanging up the phone.

Ricio sat shaking his head back and forth. Nija sat next to him and rubbed his back. He looked over at her and smiled. I didn't know what the hell the two of them had been doing, but she's got his ass wrapped around her finger. The way he stared at her was different, and she calmed him down with a touch of her hand.

"Are you okay?" she asked him.

"Yeah, I would be better once I see my little brother walk through that door." He turned to me and asked, "what the fuck is going on, Sosa."

"According to Beast, Max went to see Big Jim."

"What the hell did he do that for?" he growled.

"Beast said he went to talk Big Jim into calling a truce. Obviously, it didn't go well because Max needs a place to stay. I think Big Jim told him to get out his crib. These niggas are about to come for us hard, Ricio. We have to get a plan in motion."

"I'm already on that. I want to go out and have some fun before I attack these niggas. Once we start, we ain't stopping until all them are eating maggots and worms for dinner."

"Ricio, since you brought it up. I figured we could go out Friday to the strip club. Seeing a big booty bitch in your face would be a sight to see." Nija said staring at the side of his face.

It was like that nigga was stuck, he didn't know how to respond to what she suggested. My stupid ass started laughing uncontrollably because of the expression on his face. I loved the way Nija played that shit at the right time.

"When did you start going to the strip club?" he asked glancing at her.

"I've never been to the strip club, Ricio. I think my first time would be lit if I was there with you. What do you think?" she asked with a sneaky grin on her face.

"I don't think that would be a good idea."

"Why not, Ricio?" she chuckled.

"You would be jealous as fuck if one of them hoes give me a lap dance. I don't have time for all that catty shit." He said shaking his head no.

"I'm not you, Mauricio. That shit doesn't bother me. If I was the jealous type, it would've shown a long time ago. I don't give you or your tribe the satisfaction. Now, are we going to watch some ass shaking, pussy poppin', titty swinging hoes on Friday at Paradise Kitty?"

Ricio cut his eyes at her and I laughed again. "Shut the fuck up, Sosa! Ni, what the fuck do you know about Paradise Kitty? Yo' ass better not lie either."

"I don't know shit about it, that's why I want to go. I looked up strip clubs on the internet and that one looked clean as fuck. The dancers don't look dirty, it's in the heart of downtown, and from the videos I've seen, they know how to party. Are we going? Sosa, you want to tag along too?"

"Hell yeah, I'm in!" I said joining in on getting this nigga to commit to going.

"Aight, I'll go. The first time I see you getting upset, we leaving."

"Get upset for what? I might get me a lap dance myself, fuck you thought." She said laughing.

When Ricio was about to respond to what she said, the doorbell chimed and he got up to see who it was. He and Max walked into the family room and all jokes were put to the side. My little brother looked stressed the fuck out.

"You ready to tell us what's going on, man?"

"I want to tell y'all but it's so much to take in. I went to see Big Jim today and this muthafucka had the nerve to brag about having daddy's brains blown out. Hearing him admit it, made things real."

"Max, that's what I was trying to tell you on Monday. We know Big Jim had everything to do with Papi getting killed. Why the fuck did you think we were telling you to stay the fuck away from them? Ricio went to pay Big Jim a visit before that shit went down last night. That was the reason we rode down on them." I explained to him.

"We weren't telling you that shit to fuck up yo' money! Them niggas are snakes! Not only did they have Reese killed, they had something to do with mama dying too! There, I said that shit. You were ridin' with the enemy, Max. It was like you were saying fuck us and what they said was law. I wanted to fuck yo' ass up!" Ricio spat at him.

"I know they are not right. There's some shit that I can't reveal right now, but they ain't shit. I didn't know they had anything to do with the deaths of our parents though."

"Max, what do they have against you? What are you not telling us?" I asked.

"I can't say right now. I was threatened today and I'm not trying to lose my life." he said loudly.

I wasn't about to force him to tell us what was going on. When he is comfortable enough to tell us, he will. I could tell that he was scared, but he didn't have anything to worry about as long as he had me as a brother.

"Ricio, I want to apologize to both you and Sosa for trying to stay in their good graces. I wanted it to appear as if I was on their side to get more information from them. I went to talk to Big Jim and he refused to call off the war. He said you was a dead man walking because you disrespected him and you tried to steal from him. When I stood up for you, he told me that I had to get out his shit and he didn't give a fuck if I starved. He has basically given them the go to kill y'all."

"Bro, you don't need to apologize. I don't want you to put your life in danger for me. As far as them killing us, they better come strapped like the US muthfuckin' Army. They have to wake up early as hell to get at us with the weak muthafuckas they got on their team. Truthfully, you are the weakest of us all, I believe you will be the target. I'm gon' need you to watch your surroundings when you are out. You don't have to worry about money or any of that shit. Papí left us well off and we are opening up shop on our own. We will be having a meeting with Beast on Monday, to discuss things. Until then, I want you to lay low."

Ricio said the majority of the shit that I wanted to say and I was glad he didn't try to pressure him into telling us what he refused to let out. It was all on Max to follow the rules that were set out for him. He was going to have to live off the money that he had because there was no more going out with Shake and John John to sell packs.

"What type of bread are you talking, brah?" Max asked rubbing his hands together.

"You will learn all of that on Monday. Don't think too much about it, just know that you are good for the rest of your life. I want you to concentrate on the fact that Big Jim ain't shit, along with everybody that rolls with him. Nobody would be able to tell me they didn't know what the fuck he did. All them niggas are on my radar, everybody got a bullet with their name on it. Believe that shit. You can stay here as long as you need to, but I don't' want nobody in my shit." I said sternly.

"That's why I need my own crib. I will be looking for something next week, I'm too grown for a muthafucka to be telling me what I can and cannot do. Madysen is my girl and she can't come over, either?"

I didn't know if he was trying to start an altercation or what, but I wasn't about to feed into that shit. "Max do what you gotta do. You of all people knows I don't like for nobody to know where I lay my head. That goes for Madysen's ass too."

"What about Nija? She ain't family." He snarled.

"Nigga, she may as well be family! She's been around a long ass time. You are trying to compare some shit between a bitch yo' ass have known for a couple years, to a female that's been around since you were nine. Sit down somewhere with that hoe shit." Ricio barked at him. "Let me get up outta here. I'll let the two of y'all figure out your living arrangements. I'm going to the crib." Ricio said walking toward the door.

"See you around, Sosa. Don't forget about Friday. Bye, Max." Nija as she left out of the house.

I heard the door close and I told Max, to take the guest room that he used when he spent the night over. Picking up the remote, I turned the tv off and went to my room without saying anything else to my little brother.

Chapter 13
Nija

We pulled out of Sosa's driveway and Ricio was driving like a madman. I knew he was upset because Max used me as an example, but it wasn't that serious. As he drove, his jawline flexed constantly. I was trying my best to keep my eyes on the road because I was ready to be a backseat driver.

"Ricio, would you slow down please? I would love to live to see my twenty-second birthday." I asked as I grabbed his hand.

"Max is pissing me off because he is not telling us the whole truth. Instead of talking to us, he wants to start conflict. I don't have time for that shit, man. I'm gon' look out and be there for him, but I am no longer trying to tell him what he needs to do. He's not going to listen."

"Whatever he is going through can't be easy for him. You have to step outside of the equation to see the entire picture. Max is hurting about something. Y'all have to give him time to open up. Don't give up on him."

"You're right. I'll reach out to him and have a one on one conversation with him. By now, Floyd knows about whatever Max and Big Jim talked about. I would've paid to be the fly on the wall to hear what was said."

"Max will let y'all in on what's going on. I believe that in my heart."

He pulled into the parking lot of J &J Fish and parked. "Thank you for being here with me through all of this. What do you want out of here?"

"I don't know. I'll go in with you." I said unbuckling my seatbelt.

We got out the truck and walked toward the entrance, there was a woman staring in our direction. I didn't pay her any mind and kept walking. She headed toward us and I knew then, she was someone he knew. Her face lit up as she got closer.

"Mr. Vasquez, what are you doing in my neck of the woods?" she asked walking up to him with her arms out-stretched.

"Hey Miss Smith. I'm good and you?" he responded giving her a hug.

I stood there for a spell and decided to let them have their reunion in peace. When I took a step in the direction of the restaurant, Ricio grabbed my hand. Turning my head to glance back at him, a look of confusion was evident on my face.

"Latorra, this is my friend Nija. Nija this is Latorra."

The way he said 'this is my friend' let me know that he had more than a friendship with her. It didn't make me feel any type of way, but I wasn't about to stand there and listen to their conversation. One of these days he was going to have to make a choice.

"Hello," was all I gave her before I shrugged out of his grasp and entered the restaurant.

As I ordered our food, I glanced out the window and the two of them were all smiles. I felt my phone vibrating in my purse and I dug around to get it without taking my eyes off Ricio. Seeing my sister Nihiyah's name on the display, I answered.

"Well hello stranger. Something must be totally wrong if I'm getting a call from you."

"Nija, please. I've been busy as hell." She said.

"Busy doing what, chasing dick?"

"Oh sis, you tried it," she said laughing. "Where are you?"

"I'm at the J &J Fish on 79th with Ricio. Why what's up?"

"I was just trying to see what you were up to. We haven't hung out in a while, I miss my sister.

"Nihiyah, we ain't never hung out. Tell me what the fuck is up and stop with the bullshit. If you need some money, I don't have any." I said with an attitude.

"Damn, every time I call, I'm not asking for something! Fuck it don't worry about it. I'll talk to you later."

"Nihiyah! You better not hang up! Tell me what the fuck you want, shit."

Nihiyah was older than me but since we were younger, she always spent her money faster than she got it. I was her go to person when she needed something because she knew my mom wasn't giving her irresponsible ass anything. Now that we were adults, nothing has changed. She was still the same, money hungry and manipulative.

"I needed two hundred dollars to pay my rent that I'm short. Calling you was my last resort because mommy said she didn't have it."

"Sis. I don't have two hundred dollars. I had to pay my bills for the month. Why can't you get the money from one of the dudes you fuckin' with?" I asked with irritation.

"Because I'm asking you! Do me a favor and get it from Mauricio," she said nonchalantly.

Looking down at the phone, I couldn't believe she thought I was going to ask somebody else for money so I could give it to her. Then again, I could. My sister didn't give a fuck about anyone but herself.

"Number seventy-six," the girl behind the counter called out.

I nodded my head letting her know I heard her and went back to talking with my selfish ass sister. "Nihiyah, I will not ask Ricio or anyone else for money to give to you. When are you gonna get a damn job? I can't keep giving you my hard-earned money every month. Shit you may as well be a dependent on my fuckin' taxes."

"All you had to say was no, Nija. You could have saved your little speech for one of your welfare recipients." She said hanging up in my face.

As I walked to the counter to grab the bag that held our food, I dropped my phone in my purse. "Thank you." I called out to the girl that was prepping trays of bread. I thought about what Nihiyah said before she hung up. She needed to come down to the office and get her some damn assistance instead of downing those that's receiving it.

"Have a good day." She called back at me.

Realizing Ricio never came into the restaurant, I looked out the window and didn't see him. I got closer to the truck and realized he was sitting inside nodding his head to the music. His lady friend must've left because I didn't see her lurking. Opening the back door on the passenger side, I put the food on the floor. I got in the truck and buckled my seatbelt as Ricio put the car in reverse.

"What did you get me to eat?" he asked.

"I got you a catfish and chicken dinner with double spaghetti instead of cole slaw and two extra pieces of fish. I know what you like and dislike, Ricio."

"I know you do. Why are you all snappy and shit?" he asked.

"I'm not being snappy. I'm hungry, can we just go to my house please?"

Backing out the parking space, we made a left onto 79th street and headed eastbound to King Drive. Ricio paused at the stop sign on Indiana when a black Impala pulled on the side of us on the driver's side. I thought the car was turning but it didn't. The window came down as Ricio turned his head to look at the car. All I saw was a barrel of a big ass gun. The bullets started hitting the car and I immediately held my head between my legs to avoid getting hit.

"These muthafuckas are bold as fuck!" Ricio screamed as he pushed his foot down on the gas and peeled off.

The glass in the truck didn't shatter and Ricio didn't appear worried at all, he just kept speeding away. He cut the corner turning southbound onto to Calumet Street. He hit 80th at top speed and made a right. I knew he was trying to get to the expressway but the Impala was still behind us.

"Ricio who the fuck was that?" I asked sitting up looking out the back window. "They are still behind us! I'm so scared." I said starting to cry.

"Don't worry, Ni. We are good as long as we are in this truck, it's bulletproof. I have to shake these niggas because they will only keep coming for us."

We were coming up on State Street and the light was red. Ricio floored the truck and I prayed that we didn't get hit by another car. His head shot to the left to see what traffic looked like and headed forward full speed. Making it across the intersection gave him the time to get his gun out of his waistband. The Impala was gaining on us.

The driver rammed his car into the back of the truck but Ricio kept going. At Vincennes Street the light was red. He stopped the truck and threw it in park. Jumping out with a gun in each hand, Ricio caught the shooters off guard because they weren't expecting him to get out. He fired so many shots that I lost count.

When I looked out the rear window, I noticed both of the men were slumped over in their seats. Ricio ran back to the truck, threw the car in drive, and sped away. We got onto the expressway and my heart was pounding. He reached for his phone and made a call. The call connected and Sosa's voice came through the car speakers.

"Ricio, what's good?"

"The muthafuckas came at my head on the Nine, brah. I'm pissed because I got Ni with me. I'm trying to figure out how them niggas knew where I was. I don't even hang in that area or conduct business over there. This shit is a mystery to me."

"Who the fuck did they send for you, brah?" he asked. I could tell he was mad because he was yelling and breathing hard.

"Punk ass Luke and that pussy Rell. Them niggas won't be able to tell nobody they came at me though. I slumped both of them niggas. That's what the fuck gon' happen every muthafuckin' time they send these weak bitches for me. But I got something for em, they have really started some shit now. I'm on my way to you, I'll be there in a minute."

"Bet. Be careful Ricio, and I'll see you when you get here." He said disconnecting the call.

The ride was silent for about five miles. I looked at the guns that laid in his lap and closed my eyes. I said a silent prayer for God to make sure that Ricio and his brothers were covered. Opening my eyes, I glanced over at Ricio and he looked as if he was in deep thought.

"Ni, I'm sorry that shit happened while you were in the truck. The last thing I want is for you to be caught in the middle of my bullshit. This is between my brothers and I, along with Floyd and Big Jim. They started something that I planned to follow through with until they're all dead. I'll understand if you don't want to fuck with me until this shit is over." he said without taking his eyes off the road.

"Ricio, I'm going to stand by you because I have to look out for you, amongst other things. I am scared for all of you but y'all got to do what has to be done. Big Jim was dead wrong for what he did and revenge is top priority. I want you to come up with a solid game plan and do what you gotta do.

Those assholes would've shot and killed me if this truck didn't stop the bullets."

"That was too close to your house, Ni. I want you to stay with me until I find out how they knew where the fuck I was. It's not debatable so don't try it." he said doing ninety all the way to Sosa's house.

Ricio pulled up in Sosa's driveway and hopped out. I opened the door and stepped down out of the truck. The door to the house opened and Sosa was standing with an evil look on his face. I went to the back to get the food out the back but Ricio had already grabbed it. My appetite was gone but I hadn't eaten all day. Walking up the steps, Sosa stepped back so I could enter his home.

"Are you okay, Nija?" he asked.

I glanced up at him and nodded my head yes as I made my way to the kitchen. Ricio walked in talking to Sosa and I caught the ass end of what he was saying. "I'm killing them niggas!" he said as he sat the bag on the table in front of me. He went to the sink and washed his hands then grabbed a couple of plates transferring the food. He put mine in the microwave first and turned back to Sosa.

"Where is Max?"

"He's in the back blowing something. I asked him if they tried to contact him, he said Floyd had been calling and sending threatening messages but he hasn't responded. What's the plan, brah?" Sosa asked.

"We going to see them niggas tonight! That's what the fuck we gon' do!" Ricio yelled.

"Ricio, I don't think that's a good idea." I said in a shaky voice.

"It wasn't a good idea for them to come for me the way they did either. I'm about to show them that my heart don't pump pussy for no muthafuckin' body! They came for the right one at the wrong time," he said as the microwave chimed.

He grabbed my food and sat it in front of me along with a fork. I was having a hard time eating because I was concentrating on the call he was on. Ricio was really gearing up to go to war. Sosa was bringing out so many guns, I thought I was in a gun shop. My heart was beating fast because I didn't know what the outcome was going to be.

"Nija, eat please. I am going to take you to my crib when you're done. I need to be back when the crew gets here because I got to handle this shit." He said sitting next to me.

I hadn't eaten anything on my plate. The only thing I could do was push the food around. Ricio took the fork from my hand and scooped up some spaghetti and held it to my mouth. Accepting it, I chewed slowly but I didn't know what it tasted like. He followed it up with a piece of the perch fish that I ordered for myself. That man sat and fed me like a toddler until all of the food was gone.

"Now we can leave. You can have my food for later so you won't have to cook." He said as he got up to take the plate to the sink. "Sosa, I'm about to run Ni to the crib and I'll be back."

"Aight, cool," he said as Max walked through the patio door.

"What's the plan, Ricio? I'm going so don't say I'm not. You could've been killed and I want to lay a couple of them niggas down myself. It would be right up my alley to hit Floyd's ass."

Ricio stood thinking for a minute before he spoke. "I'm going to give you the opportunity to ride with us. Don't try to be a muthafuckin' hero, listen to the orders that we present, aight?"

"I hear ya, brah. I just want to give them niggas what they deserve and that's to die around this bitch." He said.

"Be ready when I get back." Ricio said grabbing my hand leading me to the door.

It took us twenty minutes to get to his condo, he was speeding the entire way. We pulled into the garage and he cut the truck off and got out. Following his lead, we both stood quietly waiting on the elevator. The ride up was so silent I could hear both of us breathing. Letting myself into his place, I went straight to his bedroom and sat on the end of the bed. The thought of him being shot came to mind and the tears started streaming down my cheeks.

"Ni, everything is gon' be good. Stop all that crying. The last thing I needed to worry about is you sitting here crying." He said pulling me into his arms.

"I don't want anything to happen to you, I can't help crying. Promise you are coming back." I said wailing into his chest.

He ran his hand up and down my back trying to console me. Mauricio let out a deep breath, pushed me back a little bit and lifted my chin with his finger. He lowered his head and kissed me passionately on the lips. He raised up and wiped the tears from my eyes with his thumb.

"I promise I'll be back, Ni. I don't want you to worry. I love you, ma." He took his chain from around his neck and placed it over my head. "I'll be back for that, don't try to pawn my shit before I get back." He said kissing me again before he left out the room.

I took off my shoes and crawled into his bed and snuggled with the pillow he slept on. I took in his scent and the tears soaked the pillowcase because I had a bad feeling shit was going to go wrong.

MEESHA

Chapter 14
Mauricio

Leaving my house was hard because I wanted to stay longer to make sure Ni would be alright. I couldn't though because I had shit to do. There was no way I was about to let this shit go like it was nothing. I had to clapback, it was mandatory. Letting these niggas think shit was sweet wasn't what I was going to do. Yeah, I left two of their niggas deader than a phone with no juice, but that was on them for coming for a real muthafucka.

I've been thanking my father since that first bullet made contact and bounced off the truck. I swear I forgot I was in the bulletproof truck and knew I was a goner. The only reason I was trying to get away so tough was because Nija was scared as hell. Getting her out of harm's way was my first priority. But when that nigga rammed into the back of the truck, that was it.

When I slammed on the brakes and grabbed my bitches off my lap, I saw nothing but red. Holding both of my tools in each hand, I rolled up on them niggas and emptied the clips. I didn't care who saw the shit I had done, I didn't give a damn about the police, and now, I don't give a fuck what happened next.

Arriving back to Sosa's crib, I saw the cars of all my niggas parked in the driveway and along the sidewalk. We were set on go to get at the niggas that had every intention of killing my black ass. The two punks that I had to lay down were ones that I used to school about the game. I took them under my wing out in the streets and they followed the orders of a pussy ass nigga and stopped breathing. I didn't feel bad because that's the choice they made. It was either them or me.

Turning the key in the lock, I opened the door and walked deeper into the house. The sight before me was good to see. Psycho and Felon were cleaning guns, AK was cradling his bitch Precious and rubbing her down with a cloth, Max was sitting on the couch looking paranoid, Fats were making sure the bulletproof vests were in tiptop shape, Butta was sitting back eating a damn sandwich, and Sosa was lacing up his Timbs.

Everybody was in black from head to toe. Me myself, had on all grey and I wasn't changing. I wanted them to see me coming. This was not a sneak move, this was Mauricio coming to fuck shit up.

"What up my nigga? You ready to do this shit?" Butta asked with a mouthful of food.

"Yeah, I'm ready to roll out. I thought about some shit while I was standing here watching y'all gear up for action. Their shipment is scheduled to come in today." I said looking at my watch. "It's supposed to be at the warehouse in about an hour. Floyd ain't smart enough to have changed the date and time because we are no longer working with him. That is where we are headed, whoever the fuck is there to pick up the load, that's who the fuck getting laid down. I don't care who it is." I said looking around.

"Are you saying we are going to steal their load?" Fats asked with his arms folded over his chest.

"I don't care what happens to that shit, I don't want it. The only thing I want is blood."

"Why would we go to the warehouse and hit they ass if we ain't getting shit out of it?" Butta asked.

"That's because these muthafuckas came for my head! The nigga they take orders from killed my fuckin' father! Every time I think about it, one of those niggas gon' die! Are you down or not? If not, get the fuck out, now!"

"Ricio calm down. everybody in this room has been riding with us forever. We are with you and not against you. Ain't nobody leaving because we all are rolling out of this bitch in a minute." Sosa snapped on me. "If you niggas want to take that shit, so be it. We don't need it. I won't try to stop y'all from doing whatever you want to do." He said looking at Fats.

I stood waiting to see if anyone had anything else to say. All I heard were clips snapping in place, and bullets being put in the chamber. I walked to the closet and grabbed four clips for my bitches and ejected the two empty ones before putting in the loaded ones. Slipping the extra clips into my pockets, I was ready to go find the people that wanted me dead.

Leading the way out of the crib, I went straight to the Navigator and jumped in the backseat. Fats knew that he would be driving because that's what he was best at. Don't get it wrong, his fat ass could handle a pistol with the best of them. It was his perfected driving skills that deemed him the getaway driver.

Butta was driving his own truck because that nigga wanted a place to stash all the dope he planned to take from the warehouse. He was on his own with that shit. I had no plans of stealing that bunk shit Floyd and Big Jim was selling. Once everyone was situated in the truck, Fats put the petal to the metal and I was in kill a nigga mode.

"When we get close to the warehouse, I want you to park a block away. We gon' run up on these muthafuckas and they not gon' know what the fuck hit em. I don't give a fuck who is there, I want all of y'all to go in blastin'! Won't be no talkin', none! Make all of them eat lead! This is the start of getting justice for Reese Williams! The Renegade Boys is about to run this shit. That means, we have to lay all of them down by blood and strippin' their muthafuckin' pockets! Y'all ready to do this shit?"

"Hell yeah! Justice for Reese!" Psycho yelled.

Everybody else followed suit and we were all amped up, except Max. He was quieter than a church mouse and Sosa picked up on it first. He turned around in the seat and stared at him for a couple seconds.

"Max, you good?" Sosa asked him.

"Do we have to kill them?"

I thought my hearing was going bad because I knew damned well I didn't hear him say that bullshit. This mutha-fucka was still trying to save the enemy. The same enemy that murdered our father. I was already pissed, at that moment, I was beyond the point.

"What the fuck you mean, do we have to kill them? Hell yeah, they gotta die!" I damn near jumped over the seat to punch his ass. "My question to you is, what the fuck is they holding over yo' head?" I said grabbing him by the front of his shirt. His whole demeanor was different from earlier at the house.

Nobody tried to stop me because the way he was talking, he was trying to protect them and he had nobody backing him. AK and was grilling his ass waiting to hear his response. All Max did was stared back. He still refused to tell the big secret he was holding on to.

"They don't have shit on me!" he said trying to loosen my grip. "I told y'all them niggas threatened to kill me! You want me to die, Ricio? That's what's gon' happen if I tell you what I know." He confessed.

"They can't do shit to you as long as you got us standing in front of you! I would take the muthafuckin' bullet for you and I will eliminate everybody, including Big Jim. When this shit is over, you will tell me what the fuck is going on!" I said letting him go. "Right now, it's time to make these tools clap. All I want to smell is gun smoke and all of us will live to see another day. Ain't no dying going on tonight. Get ready, because we pulling up." I said reaching for my guns and sitting down.

Fats pulled the truck along the side walk and we jumped out and made our way down the street. The warehouse was in my line of vision and there was nobody out front. That meant whoever was there was in the back.

"Psycho, AK, Fats, and Sosa, y'all go around on the left. Me, Max, Face, Butta, and Felon will go to the right." I whispered as I gave orders. "Get y'all tools ready and have them locked and loaded. We are not here to take our time, but we will make sure nothing is moving before we leave. They wanted a nigga to die, that's what we will give them for the second time today. Make it quick and simple, don't think, just shoot. I'm gon' step out first, when I shout 'Renegade, nigga' that's the cue to start letting loose."

Once everybody acknowledged the command, I pointed Sosa and his team to the left, and I led my team to the right. Creeping along the wall of the warehouse, the voices of the stupid niggas could be heard. Weed smoke could be seen and the aroma was strong. Knowing they were back there getting lit was a good sign because their reactions were going to be slow as hell. Looking behind me, I checked to see where Max was. I motioned for him to come up to where I was standing.

"Stay as close to me as possible, I don't know who is here," I whispered to him as I gripped my bitches in my hands.

Taking a deep breath, I rounded the corner with my guns drawn. As I thought, all of them hoe niggas was in a circle, not paying attention. Easy targets. "Renegade niggas!" I shouted as I let my bitches sing them a lullaby.

They never had a chance because every Renegade got a shot in. Riddling they ass with bullets felt so muthafuckin' good but I was pissed because the shit was too easy. Bodies dropped quick and fast. But there was one that ducked his way across the open space trying to get away. Noticing him running, I let off a shot that hit him in his lower leg. He collapsed on the ground and started to crawl away slowly. I took my time walking toward him. When I got closer, he turned over pleading.

"Oh shit! Please, Ricio, don't kill me man. I didn't have nothing to do with none of that shit! You know I fucks with you the long way, fam. That was Floyd and Shake! They sent Rell to get at you."

I looked down in John John's face with no remorse. If the shit he said was true, he wouldn't be at the warehouse. His ass would've left their crew when the shit went down but he didn't. His ass had to go with the rest of them.

Before I could raise my arm to pop his ass, he fired a shot into my chest. I stumbled because the pain I was feeling was intense. Looking to my right I saw John John squeezing the trigger but nothing happened. His gun jammed. I raised up squeezing the trigger shooting him in the face until he was unrecognizable.

Max ran over to where I was with his gun drawn. I was running my hand over the spot where the bullet hit. It was a good thing I had on my vest, but my chest was killing me. "Ricio, he shot you?" Max asked with wide eyes.

"Yeah, but I have on my vest. He won't be able to shoot nobody else though. I said looking down at the mess I created. Leaving his ass laying there in brain matter and blood, I walked away to make sure everybody else was good. The door to the warehouse was opened. Psycho, and Face was standing guard outside when me and Max walked up. I heard a car coming down the street and I popped a new clip into one of my pistols and aimed. Butta was pulling his truck up to the back of the warehouse and Felon was driving the Navigator.

Relaxing, I turned my head looking into the door of the warehouse and I saw Sosa coming out with three duffle bags. I told his ass I didn't want none of the weak ass drugs that was in there, his ass was hardheaded.

"I thought I told you we didn't want that shit, brah."

"Oh, this belongs to Reese. There's a shit load of product in there but these niggas about to load that up for themselves. These—" he said patting one of the bags, "are coming with us. Y'all niggas hurry up because the shipment should be here any minute. We gotta get outta here." Sosa said to Butta.

It took them ten minutes to gather enough bricks for them to make a killing and be straight for a long while. Piling back into the trucks, I glanced at the bodies that were scattered around and smiled. This was just the beginning. There would be more bloodshed in the near future.

***

Sosa, Max, and myself headed back to the suburbs while the rest of the team went to the west side. Max was sitting quietly in the back as I drove and Sosa sat chilled in the passenger seat. My mind was on what we had done and I couldn't describe the way I was feeling about it. Thinking back to the Impala the shots came out of earlier, a vision flashed in my mind. It was the same car that sped off the night my father was killed.

I'd seen that car plenty times over the years and never put two and two together until now. Briefly closing my eyes, I tried to get the vision to reappear but it didn't come back. My head starting hurting because I needed that night to come back so I could see the scene. The only thing I remembered was holding my father in my arms. Anything before that, was a blur to me.

I pulled into Sosa's driveway and before the car came to a full stop, Max bolted out. Both me and Sosa looked at him through the front window. I wanted to know badly what was on my little brother's mind, other than me almost getting shot. Watching him go inside, we sat in the car staring at the front of the house.

"We have to keep an eye on him Ricio. He's acting as if he's waiting for something to happen to him. Earlier this week he was a tough muthafucka, now he's acting all paranoid and it was before we went to get at Floyd's boys. I'll try to get him to tell me what's going on." he said glancing at me.

"I'm done trying to figure it out, brah. He's not talking but if you can get him to open up, that would be a good thing. I didn't tell you back at the warehouse, but John John got a shot off hitting me in the chest. Don't panic because it didn't get past the vest I'm wearing." I said showing him. "But on some real shit, what the fuck is in those bags?"

"Don't worry about that right now brah. Are you sure you're okay?" I shook my head yeah. "If you say so, I hope you don't complain about it later. Anyway, them stupid muthafuckas had the money for the shipment out in the open. I scooped that shit up and brought it out with me. I don't know how much is there, but I'll leave it up to you to count and divide it three ways. Floyd is really gon' be pissed that his boys got robbed and killed. His first thought is gon' be us, for sure."

The words weren't out of Sosa's mouth good before my phone chimed with a text. I quickly took it off my hip thinking it was Nija. I opened it and all I could do was chuckle. Floyd's bitch ass was texting me with his idle threats like it meant something to me.

"Check this shit out, brah. I guess his connect found the mess we left. He said we're dead." I said laughing loudly.

"Let me see." Sosa said holding his hand out for my phone. He read the text out loud, "Bitch ass niggas! This how y'all want to play? Y'all killed my fuckin' nephew! Watch yo' muthafuckin' back, Ricio. You dead, bitch!"

"Don't respond to that nigga, let him think he knows what he is talking about. I think we all need to lay low for a day. I will talk to Max and see if he wants to roll to the club with us on Friday. Go home and get some sleep and call me if you need to."

"Aight, be easy, brah. I'll call to let you know how much we banked tonight." I said dapping him up as he exited the truck.

I waited until he was in the house before I backed out of the driveway. I couldn't wait to get home. It didn't take long for me to get there because traffic was nonexistent. Pushing the button to the garage door, I pulled the truck into my secondary spot and got out. I walked to the elevator and remembered the bags that were in the backseat. Going back to the passenger side I opened the door and grabbed all three straps and slung them over my shoulder.

When I entered the condo, it was so quiet I could hear the clock ticking on the wall in the dining room. I went straight to the guest room and placed the bags in the closet. The shower was calling my name and that's where I headed. My bedroom door was open and Nija's silhouette was illuminated by the tv. Proceeding to the bed, I moved the cover from her face. She had her hand tucked under her chin with my chain clutched in it.

I bent down and kissed her softly on her forehead then went to take a shower. The hot water rained over my head and relaxed every aspect of my body. I was tired but my mind was on overload. This had been one stressful week for all of us and it would only get worse. Floyd was pissed and retaliation was on the top of his list. I knew he had already called Big Jim whining about John John, oh well. They took two from me, and I was taking as many of them muthafuckas that I could at once.

As I reached over my head grabbing the wash cloth and body wash, another vision came to my mind. I stopped suddenly to see if it would come through without the blur and it vanished. Frustration kicked in instantly because something was being revealed to me but I couldn't grasp it. Hurrying to wash myself, I rinsed and stepped out of the shower. I snatched a bath towel from the rack and wrapped it around my waist and walked out of the bathroom.

Nija was still sleeping soundly and I didn't want to wake her. Tiptoeing to the dresser, I removed a pair of shorts and a t-shirt and dressed quickly. Pulling a pair of socks onto my feet, I grabbed my phone and made my way to the guest room to count the money Sosa swiped from the warehouse. Hitting the power button on my ihome speaker, I connected my phone to the Bluetooth and went straight to Pandora.

Mc Eiht's "Straight up Menace" came through the speakers and I placed my phone on the bar and went to the closet. Removing the money counter from the shelf, I placed it on the table and went back for the bags. When I opened the first bag, there were bundles of bills that were bound together by rubber bands. As I placed the bundles on the table, I thought the bag was never going to empty.

Feeding the bills through the counter one stack at a time, it took about twenty minutes to get the sum of the money in the first bag. The total came out to two hundred thousand. When I finish counting the other two bags there was a total of seven hundred thousand dollars stacked on the table. I went back to the closet and pushed the wall to reveal the hidden safe that sat behind it. Keying in the combination, I pulled it open.

Before this lick, I probably only had seventy-five thousand dollars in the safe. Now I would be sitting on a couple hundred thousand.

I locked the safe up, replaced the wall, and sat at my desk. With my fingers intertwined under my chin, I looked to my left and saw the disc with my name on it. I hadn't listened to it when Beast gave it to me but I thought that moment would be the perfect time to do so. Since visiting the cemetery, my dad had been on my mind heavily. Taking the disc out of the case, I inserted it into my laptop after powering it on. I grabbed my earphones and placed them on my ears and waited.

"Mauricio, I know it's surprising to hear my voice right now. By this time, you are a grown ass man. Happy birthday, nigga! Congratulations on your completion of college, I have faith that you did that. I want you to be me when it comes to your brothers, beat their ass if they ain't doing right. I give you my permission. I know Sosa can handle himself, it's Max I need you to keep an eye on.

I know Beast let you hear the disc as I revealed everything I had set up for you and your brothers. I told you about the storage locker, let me tell you about the deposit box. There is an envelope with account numbers in it for you and Sosa. Max has one too but he is not to get his until he turns twenty-one. Outside of the drugs that I have stashed for y'all, there is a lot of money that you now have. You are an instant millionaire and you didn't have to do shit for it. I want you to be smart son, don't be in the streets flossin', throwing money around, and acting untouchable. There are a lot of envious niggas and bitches in this world waiting to catch you slipping because they want what you have. Take my situation into considera-tion. The niggas that got me, were so called friends, be care-ful.

Speaking of friends. I don't know if you and Sosa still hang around Fred—"

I frowned when he mentioned Psycho's government name and paused the disc. At that moment I prayed he wasn't going to say Psycho was a snake because that meant I would have to kill my best friend. Taking a deep breath to calm my nerves before I jumped to any conclusions, I pressed the play button and sat back in the chair. My dad's voice boomed out once again after I backed the recording up a little bit.

"I don't know if you and Sosa still hang around Fred, but what I'm about to say may mess up y'all friendship. Rodney was in on the shit with Big Red and Floyd. The reason I didn't disclose that information on the other recording is because I want you to see what your friend knows. I want you to test his loyalty to you and have him confront his bitch ass father about the situation. That will let you know where you stand with him.

Also, there's Slim. Slim was my nigga and he knows more about Big Jim and Floyd's plans. He was one of my loyal customers that was always hanging around listening as well as smoking that shit. All you have to do is give him a pack and he will sing like a bird. I don't want you to do that though, son. I want you to help him by getting him into rehab. Slim deserves a second chance at life. Clean him up, he is your trump card.

You are a replica of me and I knew once you heard what went down, you would be out for blood. I hope you understand that once you attacked, you've started a war. I'm not worried about you not being able to protect yourself, that's automatic with your bloodline. But I have to say this again, watch out for the snakes. You would never know who it is if you don't pay close attention. Remember, snakes shed their skin on the regular, they can put on many faces.

Last but not least, I want you to know that I'm watching every move you make. I love you Ricio and don't you ever forget that. I didn't choose the way my life ended, it was forced upon me. If it was my choice to live forever, I'd still be there. But I'm living through you now, and you have me as your greatest leader. Don't try so hard to see the things in your mind, relax and things will be revealed when the time is right. I love you son, I'm out."

I turned the laptop off and set the earphones on top of it. Making a mental note to holla at Psycho and Slim, I turned off the light and closed the door. I entered my bedroom and crawled in the bed behind Nija and fell asleep.

Rest was what I needed because I was sleep before my head hit the pillow. I felt Nija snuggling closer to me with her ass against my joint. I was too tired to even attempt to slip into her honey pot. The darkness behind my lids was peaceful and relaxing. My mind had slowed down tremendously and I was finally allowing my body to rest. I don't know how long it lasted but the vision of me and my dad came into view vividly.

My dad was revealing the midnight black BMW that he had bought for me as a graduation gift. I was walking around whistling and rubbing my hands together as I inspected my new ride.

"Thanks, Papí. I can get all the ladies in this whip." I said laughing.

"You can do what ya like, but you better strap the fuck up." he shot back looking down at his phone and the smile fell from his lips. "Aye, tell ya mama I'll be back. I have some business I need to take care of."

"Can I roll with you? I'm not ready to go in the house and all the graduation parties aren't until tomorrow."

"Yeah, come on."

We jumped in his Navigator and backed out of the drive-way. He hit the expressway and we were heading to the city. His phone kept going off but he didn't answer it. I kept looking down at it because he had thrown it in the cup holder facing me when he got in the truck. Big Jim's name kept popping up on the screen, but I didn't tell my dad who it was.

We were on a street called Washtenaw and he was cruis-ing along. I had never been on this side of the city before so I had no clue where we were. There were niggas standing on almost every corner trying to see who was in the truck. As we stopped at a stop sign, a woman with a skirt riding up her ass stepped up to the truck and tapped on the window. My daddy ignored her and pulled off.

He drove a couple blocks and parked by a building that looked abandoned. "I want you to stay in the truck and don't get out no matter what happens, okay?"

I shook my head yeah and he opened the door and got out. As I watched him walk up to someone that was leaning against the wall, I saw my dad pointing his finger in the guy's face. it was dark as hell on that end of the street so all I could see was the guy's body build. He pushed my dad making him stumble back a little bit. My dad pulled what I noticed was a gun from his waistband and shoved the guy back against the wall.

Leaning forward so I could see what was going on, an-other person crept behind my dad and pointed something to his head. All I saw was a flash along with a loud boom. My dad fell to the ground and I fumbled with the door for a few seconds before I was able to open it. Both of the guys ran off as his body hit the pavement. I ran as fast as I could to my dad's side, he had a pool of blood seeping under his head.

I fell to my knees and cradled his head with my hand. The hole that I felt was the size of a golf ball and it felt like wet noodles in my palm. Blood was oozing out of his mouth and his chest was moving up and down very fast. With every second that passed, his chest started rising slower. I knew he was about to die so I started talking to him.

"Papí, you gotta fight! Don't leave me, please!" his eyes started closing and I shook his head back and forth. "No, don't close your eyes!" I yelled in his face.

I glanced around to see if there was anyone that could help me. My eyes landed on a black Impala that sat in the middle of the street. The person in the driver's seat just sat there watching. It was Rodney. He drove away from the scene fast, leaving me on the dark street by myself with my dad lying dead in my arms.

I looked down at my dad's chest and it was no longer moving. He had stopped breathing and all of his bodily fluids were making a path on the sidewalk. I continued holding him as my tears fell upon his face.

"Ricio! Ricio! Wake up baby." I heard Nija yelling while trying to shake me awake.

I opened my eyes and I was sitting straight up with a pillow cradled in my hands the same way I was holding my dad that night. My tears had dropped on top of it the same exact way it happened in my dream. Staring at Nija, I pulled her in my arms and cried like a baby. She didn't ask any questions, she just held me in her arms tightly.

MEESHA

Chapter 15
Sosa

I had been sitting on pens and needles trying to figure out when Max left the house yesterday morning. I stayed up damn near the whole night after we laid them niggas down at the warehouse because I was worried about Max. He wouldn't tell me what the fuck was going on with him so I badgered his ass like a witness on the stand. Which now I feel was too much for him because when I woke up, he was gone.

I've been out looking for him as well as calling his phone without him answering or calling back. All I wanted was to hear his voice so I would know he was alright. Mauricio was mad because he shot a text to Floyd asking if he'd seen Max, and his bitch ass only laughed as a reply. Deep down in my heart I knew he was alive but I wanted to hear for myself.

We had three hours before Mauricio's party was set to start and it was too late to cancel. There was no way we would be able to have a good time with our little brother missing. I grabbed my phone and dialed Max's number for the hundredth time and was surprised when it was answered.

"What up, brah?" he said nonchalantly.

"Where are you, Max? I've been calling you over and over again since yesterday morning!" I said angrily into the phone.

"My bad. I'm with Madysen, I needed to get away. Tell Ricio I'm still meeting y'all tonight for his birthday." He said too calmly.

"With the shit that's going on, I thought they killed yo' ass, Max. You scared the fuck outta us! What happened to laying low?"

"And I said, my fault. I didn't think I needed permission to make love to my girl. I am laying low, with Madysen. Look, I'll see y'all at the club." He said hanging up.

I sat on the bed for a few minutes and the conversation ran through my mind several times. Something was off with Max. He didn't sound like himself. Getting up off the bed, I went to the closet and took my outfit out for the night. The pair of white jeans I picked out, along with a white button down shirt was my outfit for the tonight. I was going for a debonair look before everything hit the fan. So, I had to settle for comfortable just in case Floyd decided to show up on some revenge type shit.

Walking to the bathroom with my phone in hand, I dialed up Nija. I listened as it rang numerous times before she answered. "Hey, brother. Have you heard from Max?"

"Yes, he said that he would see us at the club. He's at Madysen's house. He claims he needed to get away but he didn't sound like himself. Whatever is weighing on his mind, is eating him up. I will see for myself when he gets to the club. Is Mauricio getting ready?"

"He's in the shower. Sosa, he refused to wear white though. It's like he is anticipating something to happen tonight. Ricio will be dressed in all black from head to toe. Please tell me nothing will happen tonight." I was quiet for a moment because I didn't want to lie to her. "Sosa, promise me nothing will go down," she said in a whiny voice.

"Nija, I can't make that promise. I really don't know what's bound to happen to be honest. We will go out, celebrate bro's birthday, and have a good time. That's all we can do."

"Who is that on the phone, Ni?" Ricio said in the background.

"It's Sosa. He heard from Max and he will meet us at the club."

"That's good, bro. We will see you in a minute. Until then, let my girl get herself together, nigga!" he said laughing.

"Your girl? When the hell did that happen?" Nija asked.

"Act like you don't kn

"Okay, I'll let y'all wor

I said hanging up.

Turning the water on in the

the counter and undressed. The

pretty fast and it was like a sauna

and turned the cold water on a little

ping into the shower the water casca

the beat of the water relaxed my mind.

Retaliation was on my mind heavily.

knew that night was going to be when the

held my head down and I heard the voice o

"get ready to fight back. Focus on Max. Keep h

sight at all times." To me, that sounded like a wa

from heaven and it touched every nerve in my bod

I washed quickly and got out of the shower. An

a half had passed before I knew it. I dressed quickly an

my Timbs from the box in the closet and slipped my fe

them. Walking to my gun closet, I stood back examining

tool to decide which ones were hanging out with me. I decid

to take my silver and black Nina's with the extended clips fo

the ride. I grabbed four extra clips, each holding thirty-two

bullets each. If anything happened, I would be ready.

Placing my guns in the holster along with the clips, I look up at the clock and it was nine o'clock. I had already talked to security that would be at the door and they knew my entire team would be packing heat. The money I dished out to get inside strapped, wasn't shit to me. I had to make sure we were all safe.

I decided to drive my BMW to the club because I wanted to have a fast car under my ass. Walking to the garage, I inserted the key and backed out once the door went up fully. I hit the team with a text letting them know I was on my way to

ow, Ni:"
k that out. I'll holla at y'all later."

shower, I placed my phone on
steam filled the bathroom
ithin minutes. I reached in
bit to add warmth. Step-
ed down my body and

For some reason I
y would attack. I
f my father say,
m in your eye-
ning coming
.
hour and
d pulled
t into
ach
ed

was al-

took

vas

y

VIP
Jr. There's
.own behind the
.ght. You know we go
.I I see them nigga's, I will
. nave the phone on vibrate."
.preciate all that you've done to make
.or Ricio. Also, for having our back through
. got going on. I'm hoping nothing pops off be-
. don't want nothing to fuck up this night."

"Go on in and enjoy the night, fam. Enjoy your brother's birthday." He said walking to the door to let me in.

When I entered the club, the music was bumping through the speakers. There were nigga's surrounding the stage watching a dark-skinned beauty take her clothes off seductively to Tanks "When We." Gyrating her hips to the beat, she turned her back to the crowd and bent over. Her pussy looked like a wolf knuckle from the back. She dropped down into a split and popped her ass cheeks one at a time to the beat of the song.

My ass was mesmerized and I didn't hear anyone come up behind me.

"Oh yeah, nephew, I see right now all this pussy is gonna have y'all off ya game." Sin laughed in my ear while draping her arm over my shoulder. "I want you to enjoy the show, but at the same time, pay attention."

I glanced at her and laughed, "Man this is gon' be hard, but it's doable. I don't think those nigga's coming through here. Where's Beast?"

"He's in the cut and can see everything from his position. I came over to let you know that Max just came in. He's sitting in VIP with Madysen. He doesn't look too happy to be here, Sosa."

"I'll go over to see if he's okay. This muthafucka filled up quick! Let me hit Nija up to see where they are. I need the DJ to be ready when he walks in. Thanks for looking out for us, Sin. I appreciate both you and Beast."

"Get outta here with that soft shit, y'all about to own this city! Act like it, nigga! Nah, I wouldn't have it any other way. We family and that's what family does. Go check on your brother, I'm gonna go mingle a little bit."

Watching Sin walk away in her white Vera Wang pants suit with a silver bustier underneath. Her pants were hugging her ass right and I got lost in the sight before me. I took my eyes off her when I felt my phone vibrate on my hip. Taking it out, I had a text from Beast.

Beast: Yo' ass lookin' at the wrong bitch! There's plenty of hoes around this muthafucka, that one is mine, nigga.

I didn't know where his ass was, but I got caught red handed lusting over his woman. I threw my thumb up in acknowledgement, wherever he was he saw that shit. Heading to the VIP lounge, my phone went off again and it was Nija.

183

Nija: We are ten minutes away, get ready.

Turning back around I went to the DJ booth to let him know Ricio would be there shortly. He spoke into his head-piece and informed Sam to let him know when he got to the door. I thanked him and went to talk to Max quickly. When I got to the area, Madysen was sitting next to him glancing around the club while he sipped Hennessy.

"What up, brah? How ya doing?"

"I'm good. You did the damn thing for bro. He is gon' be pissed because you know he hates surprises." He said as he stood and gave me a brotherly hug.

"He will be okay once these hoes start shaking all that ass in his face. How you doing Madysen?" I asked hugging her.

At that moment Psycho and the rest of the team waltzed into our section ready to turn up. "Man, look at all these fine ass bitches up in here!" Felon said two stepping to the beat.

Butta grabbed one of the dancers and whispered in her ear and she smiled as she nodded her head and left. Everybody filled their glasses and the party was in full effect. Two minutes later a group of naked bad bitches strolled in and the entertainment was in place.

I watched everyone having a good time, except Max. He was still sitting in the same spot downing drinks. Sitting next to him, I whispered in his ear, "brah, what's going on?" he shook his but I wasn't believing that for a moment. "Something is going on because you downing those drinks fast as fuck. Talk to me."

"Sosa, I'm just trying to have a good time for my brother's birthday. I'm cool." he said tossing back the cognac that was in his glass.

"Slow down for me, okay? I need everybody on their shit in case something pops off."

His eyes shifted away from me and he nodded. I didn't know what the fuck he was going through but I would be keeping an eye on him. The DJ changed the music and Jay Z's "Takeover" blared through the speakers. That was the cue that Ricio was entering the building. We all rushed to the front entrance and he walked in just as Nija said, sporting all black. The only thing that glistened was the diamond RB charm that hung from his neck.

"Happy muthafuckin' birthday Ricio! We 'bout to turn up in this bitch!" the DJ yelled into the mic.

Ricio looked down at Nija and mushed her in the head before he grabbed her in a big hug. Sis was representing like a supermodel in a short white off the shoulder dress with six-inch green stilettos that made her legs appear long and sexy.

"Nigga how the fuck didn't I see this shit? I knew something was up because Ni don't do strip clubs," he said speaking in my ear as we hugged.

"I had this planned before everything happened. I was going to cancel everything but decided not to. We are about to enjoy ourselves before we wreck shit out here."

"No doubt, let's turn up!" he said letting me go.

Max walked up and shook up with Ricio and went right back to VIP. I grabbed Psycho by the arm, pulling him to the side. "I'm going to need you to help me keep an eye on Max. I don't know what's going on with him but something ain't right."

"I got you, fam. He will be alright. We got big booty bitches waiting for us in the lounge, it's time to check out the eye candy."

Ricio looked down at Nija and she smiled at him grabbing his hand. We walked back to our section and the party was lit. I walked to the food table because I hadn't eaten anything all day. Ricio and Nija walked to the couch and sat down. Piling my plate, I sat at the table with Max and Madysen. The fish I chose was seasoned really well.

"Brah, I think you should grab something to eat before you drink anything else."

"I'm not hungry," he said throwing another shot back.

I looked up and saw Nija showing out. She was grinding on Ricio's lap like she was one of the strippers in the building. The smile that graced his lips were bigger than Mt. Everest. He had his arms outstretched and he was having the time of his life. I couldn't do anything but laugh at the two of them.

The whole crew had a bitch in their lap except me and Max. I finished my food and poured me a drink and sat back observing shit. A Haitian beauty walked toward me. Her hips swayed with every step she took in my direction. Her dark complexion was smooth and her hair framed her face show-casing her beauty. The only thing she wore was pasties on her nipples and a thong.

Mocha was her name in my head and shawty was bad! She turned her back to me and her ass cheeks swallowed the fuck out of the string that held her thong together. As she made her ass clap together like it was giving me a standing ovation, I was stuck. Mocha grabbed my hands and placed them on her waist. That gave me the okay to palm her ass.

I reached into my pocket and pulled out the money that I brought to splurge. Putting a couple hundred in her waistband, she started gyrating on my pipe. He woke up instantly and I had to adjust him before he bust through my pants. My phone vibrated and I snatched it off my hip and checked the message.

Beast: We got company. Stay alert!

Staring at the text I was about to respond when another came through from Sin.

Sin: Floyd, Red, and Shake are in the building. I got them in my line of vision. Heads up.

A third text came through and it was from Sam.

Sam: Bitch niggas snuck in when I got off the door. My bad, fam. I'm watching them watch y'all. Keep ya eyes open.

This was what I hoped and prayed wouldn't happen. This was supposed to be the night to celebrate but now it was about to turn into something else. I turned to Max and leaned in so he could hear what I was saying.

"Floyd and his crew's here. I need you to stop drinking because shit is about to get real, brah. You strapped right?"

"Nah, I didn't bring it inside with me. It's in my ride." He responded.

He knew what the fuck was going on and he out here naked as fuck without his tool. I was pissed off at him but he's lucky I decided to bring a third pistol with me. I took the .25 out of my ankle strap and handed it to him. "Here, take this."

"Sosa, I'm not worried about shit, I'm here to have fun. There's too many muthafuckas in here for them to start a gunfight in this club. We cool, calm down."

My phone went off again, it was Beast. When I read the message, I knew shit was about to go amiss.

Beast: We are outnumbered. About fifteen more members of his crew just showed up.

I jumped up and moved Mocha off me. "I'm sorry miss lady, I have to handle something." I rushed over to Ricio and he saw the panic in my eyes. He stood meeting me halfway along with Psycho and the rest of the team.

"Sosa what's going on?" Ricio asked.

"Floyd and his crew's in the building. There's about twenty of them, brah. We are outnumbered, we gotta go!"

"We ain't about to run from these niggas! We are leaving out of here because I don't want innocent people getting hurt over this shit. But we won't run from no mufuckin' body!

Butta get Nija and Madysen and lead them out the nearest emergency exit. Psycho, I want you to hold on to Max, don't let him out yo' sight! The rest of y'all let's go." Ricio said walking out of the lounge.

Before he could leave, Nija grabbed his arm. "Ricio what's going on?"

"Nija, don't ask no questions. Go with Butta and get in the car and leave!" he said handing her the keys to his car.

"Ricio, no—" she cried out.

"This is not a debate, Ni. I want you to leave because I don't need anything happening to you. Come on now, you are wasting valuable time. Go home and I will be there as soon as I'm done."

She was crying hard as Butta grabbed her arm and guided her and Madysen to the emergency exit. The look on Ricio's face was a mixture of sadness and anger. It went to straight rage after Nija left out of the exit door.

He stormed to the main floor and we were right behind him. My phone started ringing and I answered it. Holding my finger to me ear so I could hear, Beast's voice boomed through the phone.

"What the fuck are y'all doing? Don't be stupid, Sosa!"

"Ricio ain't backing down! I'm not letting him go into this alone, bring yo' ass out of hiding nigga." I said hanging up.

I saw Sin easing her way to the bar where Floyd and his guys were. They saw us coming and headed for the main entrance. Something was in motion and I hated I didn't know what. Ricio picked up his pace to get to the exit when a stream of gunshots could be heard coming from outside. My heart dropped because Butta and the girls were out there.

All of us rushed to the door at the same time. Max pushed his way through and bolted out the door first before Ricio could snatch him back. When he emerged, gunshots followed forcing Ricio to dive out of the way. Snatching his banga from his hip, he returned fire across the street but was no match for Floyd and his crew. He hurried to find cover but his bitch never stopped clapping.

Pulling both of my guns from my holster, I stepped outside blasting. The rest of our crew must've used other doors to get in on the action because it sounded like WWII around that bitch. Sin appeared out of nowhere popping off her tool hitting one of them niggas with a headshot while taking cover behind a car.

Beast had set up on the side of the building and let loose as well. The smell of gun powder filled the air along with the screams from the inside of the club as well as on the street.

"Get them muthafuckas, they trying to roll out!" I heard Psycho yell over the gunfire.

Aiming both of my guns, I pulled the trigger and nothing happened, my clip was empty. "Fuck!" I hurried to reload and fired at the cars they were rushing to get in. One of them ran around the car and I sniped his ass before he could get in. The driver peeled out with the back door open.

The sounds of their tires screeching loudly were heard as they sped down the street. Madysen's screams brought me back to what was going on behind me. It would forever be embedded in my mind along with the sight of my little brother laying in his own blood.

"Wake up Max! Oh my god, Max please wake up baby!" she said shaking him to get a response.

Ricio and I got to Max at the same time and I fell to my knees. Madysen was holding on to him tightly and I couldn't get her to let him go.

"Madysen! We have to get him to the hospital. You have to let him go, ma." Ricio screamed in her face.

She wasn't trying to hear anything he was saying because she continued shaking Max. I pried her arms loose and Ricio scooped Max up in his arms. There was no time to waste waiting on an ambulance. Nija had brought the car to the front of the club and Ricio ran straight for it placing Max in the backseat. I crawled in the back with him laying his head in my lap as Ricio took over the driver's seat.

Speeding to the hospital that was five minutes away, Max's breathing was slowly fading. "Drive this muthafucka, bro! He's not doing too good." I screamed at Ricio. "Hold on Max, we almost there, man. Just hold on for me.

Ricio parked in the front of the hospital and jumped out. "Help! We need some help out here!" Ricio screamed while snatching the door open to grab Max out.

***

Carrying my brother from the car drenched in blood, had me madder than a muthafucka. I couldn't believe Floyd pulled that pussy shit. The coward was ready to play target practice with our ass. Max wasn't thinking when he ran out the door without caution. They better hope he pulled through, it didn't matter because they just signed their own death certificate.

"Sosa, yo' mufuckin' ass better hold him up! Muster up some strength from somewhere and don't drop him!" Ricio screamed at me.

"I got him, bro, I got him! Aye, somebody come over here and help my brother! Don't just stand there, get a fuckin' doctor!" I screamed as we rushed through the hospital doors.

Doctors and nurses jumped into action getting Max on a stretcher. They rushed him to the back while administering oxygen and cutting his clothes off along the way. The doctors vanished behind the operating doors with Max and we tried to follow but was stopped by a fine ass nurse.

"Y'all can't go back there. I'm gonna need y'all to fill out some paperwork, then the police wanna ask y'all some questions." She said while twisting her neck and popping the gum she was chewing on.

This bitch was beautiful but became uglier the more she opened her mouth. How can you be so damn cute but has the ghetto-ism down to a science? She could at least tone that shit down while at work. Being a nurse requires professionalism, something she obviously didn't possess.

"Ricio looked shawty up and down with the screw face. "Bitch, ain't nobody worried about no muthafuckin' paperwork. That's my little brother they just took back there fighting for his life, but you talking about paperwork? Get the fuck outta my face before I fuck yo' ass up! I don't want to hear shit else, man." He said walking away from the nurse.

I followed him to the waiting room where he sat with his head in his hands. I was praying hard for Max to pull through. The fact I was just talking to him less than an hour ago, was fuckin' with me. "Why would he run out the door the way he did?" Was the question that kept running through my mind.

Ricio raised his head and his eyes seemed unfocused. I touched him on the shoulder and he automatically pulled out on me. Both of his Nina's on point, right in the waiting room of the hospital.

"Put that shit down, nigga! What the fuck, twelve all through this bitch! I know you mad brah, but don't get ya'self caught up, not right now." I pleaded.

Holstering his weapons, Ricio grabbed his head with his hands and let out a frustrating growl. "Grrrrrrrrrrr! Fuck! This shit ain't right man! He didn't deserve this shit! It was me they were after, I was the one they had beef with! That lil nigga was riding hard for them bitches and they hit him hard!" he cried with tears rolling down his face. "Papi told me to watch him, Sosa! I failed him, brah. I failed him because I didn't keep, Max safe." He continued to wail.

I grabbed my big brother and held him tight. He was crying for Max, Papi, and our mother. Something that he hadn't done in the past four years. Me on the other hand, couldn't shed a tear. My mind was on killa mode and I just had to make sure my brother was going to be alright.

The automatic doors opened and Psycho and the rest of the homies walked in followed by Beast, Sin, and Madysen. When I saw Psycho, I rushed up to him and grabbed him in the collar pushing him into the glass.

"I asked you to make sure he was good! How was he able to get to that door like that, Psych?" I screamed in his face.

"Sosa, you not about to try to pin this shit on me! We were all there going after them niggas! None of us knew they was going to shoot him like that! They even got Butta. He gone Sosa!"

Releasing his shirt, I started shaking from the inside out. I didn't think anyone else was shot. Butta was taking Nija and Madysen outside to get them out of the line of fire in case something happened.

"Where is Nija?" I asked looking around.

"Nija is sitting over there," Ricio said pointing to the chairs where he was seated a few minutes ago. "She was in the car with us when we brought Max in." My mind was gone that badly that I didn't know who was in the car with us. Nija was sitting by herself rocking back and forth ringing her hands together.

Ricio still had tears running down his face and his nose flared wide. "I'm killing any and everything associate with them niggas. Ain't no more talking, threatening, saying what we gon' do. I'm out for blood!" Ricio said loudly.

"Aye, he gon' be good fam. He gon' be good." Felon said repeatedly as if he was trying to convince himself. "Regardless of the outcome, we will find them and they gon' wish they were dead. If don't nobody know how we get down, they do."

"We need to go outside." Beast said. "There's too many cops in this muthafucka for y'all to be talking like that." Before we could head out, the ghetto nurse walked over smacking on that damn gum.

"The doctor will be out shortly to talk to y'all." She said with her head down and walked away. She didn't look anyone in the eyes. I guess the way Ricio cussed her out made her nervous.

A black doctor walked in our direction with a grim expression. I didn't want to jump to conclusions so I gritted my teeth as he approached. He had his hands deep inside his scrub pants and his stride slowed tremendously.

"Hello, I'm Dr. Jacobs and I am the surgeon that worked on your friend that was brought in." he introduced himself.

"That's my brother, how is he?" Ricio asked.

"Your brother suffered a total of thirteen gunshot wounds. He was shot five times in his lower back, four times in his legs, once in his shoulder, once in the neck, and twice in the chest." the doctor explained.

"Ok, how is he? I mean, he is gon' be alright, ain't he?" Ricio asked damn near holding his breath waiting on a reply.

"Hell yeah, he okay, bro. He ain't going out like that! Let the man finish telling us what we need to know" I was silently praying that my words held some type of truth.

"Well he lost a lot of blood from being shot multiple times. We tried to stop the bleeding but the bullet that pierced his neck, clipped a main artery. We couldn't save—"

I started yelling at the top of my lungs. The tears finally found their way down my face. "Damn doc! I know yo ass ain't about to stand there and fix yo lips to say you couldn't save my little brother! You can't tell me no shit like that, man. You can say anything else, but not that. Please!"

My voice got weaker with the thought of what the doctor was about to say. Everybody circled around me trying to calm me down. Nija came over and stood with Ricio holding him around his waist. Beast draped his around my shoulder because he knew how I feel about my brothers. He gave the doctor the go ahead to continue what he was saying while shaking his head with tears in his eyes.

"I'm sorry to say this but as I was saying, we couldn't stop the bleeding from his neck and he lost too much blood. Your brother succumbed from his injuries."

When he confirmed that Max had died, Nija screamed loudly and buried her face in Ricio's chest. He stood silently while consoling Nija with tears running down his face. All of the guys were holding their heads down trying to hide their tears. Sin was crying against the wall and Beast was at her side making sure she would be okay. Madysen collapsed on the floor and nurses rushed over to attend to her. I was ready to blow shit up!

My chest was hurting because I was fighting the urge to breakdown. I couldn't believe I would never see my brother again. All week I had been yelling at him, beating his ass, and being in his face. I wish I would've spent that time telling him how much I loved him.

"I give my deepest condolences to you guys" the doctor said before he walked away.

Running out of the hospital, I fell to my knees and cried like a baby. "Why God, why? He was just a kid!" I cried.

Ricio got down on his knees wrapping his arms around me. "Brah, it's gon' be okay. We gon' get them muthafuckas for this."

The tears that flowed from my eyes were replaced with pure hatred. "Find them muthafuckas! If you find them before me, bring 'em to me alive! If we can't find them, we gon' paint this bitch red until we do! I don't give a fuck if we have to kill mama's, daddy's, sister's, or brothers. Shit, kill the whole muthafuckin' family, I don't give a fuck! That's what the fuck that nigga did to mine! Y'all think they call this city Chiraq, this bitch about to turn into the muthafuckin' Hiroshima!" I said pulling my tools from the holster.

To be continued...
Renegade Boys 2
Coming Soon

Submission Guideline

Submit the first three chapters of your completed manuscript to ldpsubmissions@gmail.com, subject line: Your book's title. The manuscript must be in a .doc file and sent as an attachment. Document should be in Times New Roman, double spaced and in size 12 font. Also, provide your synopsis and full contact information. If sending multiple submissions, they must each be in a separate email.

Have a story but no way to send it electronically? You can still submit to LDP/Ca$h Presents. Send in the first three chapters, written or typed, of your completed manuscript to:

LDP: Submissions Dept
Po Box 870494
Mesquite, Tx 75187

DO NOT send original manuscript. Must be a duplicate.

Provide your synopsis and a cover letter containing your full contact information.

Thanks for considering LDP and Ca$h Presents.

Coming Soon from Lock Down Publications/Ca$h Presents

BOW DOWN TO MY GANGSTA

By **Ca$h**

TORN BETWEEN TWO

By **Coffee**

BLOOD STAINS OF A SHOTTA **III**

By **Jamaica**

STEADY MOBBIN II

By **Marcellus Allen**

BLOOD OF A BOSS **V**

By **Askari**

LOYAL TO THE GAME **IV**

By **T.J. & Jelissa**

A DOPEBOY'S PRAYER **II**

By **Eddie "Wolf" Lee**

IF LOVING YOU IS WRONG… **III**

LOVE ME EVEN WHEN IT HURTS

By **Jelissa**

TRUE SAVAGE **V**

By **Chris Green**

BLAST FOR ME **III**

ROTTEN TO THE CORE **III**

By **Ghost**

ADDICTIED TO THE DRAMA **III**

By **Jamila Mathis**

LIPSTICK KILLAH **III**

CRIME OF PASSION **II**

By **Mimi**

WHAT BAD BITCHES DO **III**

KILL ZONE

By **Aryanna**

THE COST OF LOYALTY **II**

By **Kweli**

SHE FELL IN LOVE WITH A REAL ONE **II**

By **Tamara Butler**

LOVE SHOULDN'T HURT **III**

RENEGADE BOYS **II**

By **Meesha**

CORRUPTED BY A GANGSTA **III**

By **Destiny Skai**

A GANGSTER'S CODE III

By **J-Blunt**

KING OF NEW YORK II

By **T.J. Edwards**

CUM FOR ME **IV**

By **Ca$h & Company**

GORILLAS IN THE BAY

De'Kari

THE STREETS ARE CALLING

Duquie Wilson

Available Now

RESTRAINING ORDER **I & II**

By **CA$H & Coffee**

LOVE KNOWS NO BOUNDARIES **I II & III**

By **Coffee**

RAISED AS A GOON I, II, III & IV

BRED BY THE SLUMS I, II, III

BLAST FOR ME I & II

ROTTEN TO THE CORE I II

By **Ghost**

LAY IT DOWN **I & II**

LAST OF A DYING BREED

BLOOD STAINS OF A SHOTTA I & II

By **Jamaica**

LOYAL TO THE GAME

LOYAL TO THE GAME II

LOYAL TO THE GAME III

By **TJ & Jelissa**

BLOODY COMMAS I & II

SKI MASK CARTEL I II & III

KING OF NEW YORK

By **T.J. Edwards**

IF LOVING HIM IS WRONG…I & II

By **Jelissa**

WHEN THE STREETS CLAP BACK I & II III

By **Jibril Williams**

A DISTINGUISHED THUG STOLE MY HEART I II & III

LOVE SHOULDN'T HURT I II

RENEGADE BOYS

By **Meesha**

A GANGSTER'S CODE I & II

By J-Blunt

PUSH IT TO THE LIMIT

By **Bre' Hayes**

BLOOD OF A BOSS **I, II, III & IV**

By **Askari**

THE STREETS BLEED MURDER **I, II & III**

THE HEART OF A GANGSTA I II& III

By **Jerry Jackson**

CUM FOR ME

CUM FOR ME 2

CUM FOR ME 3

An **LDP Erotica Collaboration**

BRIDE OF A HUSTLA **I II & II**

THE FETTI GIRLS **I, II& III**

CORRUPTED BY A GANGSTA I & II

By **Destiny Skai**

WHEN A GOOD GIRL GOES BAD

By **Adrienne**

A GANGSTER'S REVENGE **I II III & IV**

THE BOSS MAN'S DAUGHTERS

THE BOSS MAN'S DAUGHTERS II

THE BOSSMAN'S DAUGHTERS III

THE BOSSMAN'S DAUGHTERS IV

THE BOSS MAN'S DAUGHTERS **V**

RENEGADE BOYS

A SAVAGE LOVE **I & II**

BAE BELONGS TO ME

A HUSTLER'S DECEIT I, II

WHAT BAD BITCHES DO I, II

By **Aryanna**

A KINGPIN'S AMBITON

A KINGPIN'S AMBITION **II**

I MURDER FOR THE DOUGH

By **Ambitious**

TRUE SAVAGE

TRUE SAVAGE II

TRUE SAVAGE **III**

TRUE SAVAGE **IV**

By **Chris Green**

A DOPEBOY'S PRAYER

By **Eddie "Wolf" Lee**

THE KING CARTEL **I, II & III**

By **Frank Gresham**

THESE NIGGAS AIN'T LOYAL **I, II & III**

By **Nikki Tee**

GANGSTA SHYT **I II &III**

By **CATO**

THE ULTIMATE BETRAYAL

By **Phoenix**

BOSS'N UP **I , II & III**

By **Royal Nicole**

I LOVE YOU TO DEATH

MEESHA

By Destiny J

I RIDE FOR MY HITTA

I STILL RIDE FOR MY HITTA

By **Misty Holt**

LOVE & CHASIN' PAPER

By **Qay Crockett**

TO DIE IN VAIN

By **ASAD**

BROOKLYN HUSTLAZ

By **Boogsy Morina**

BROOKLYN ON LOCK I & II

By **Sonovia**

GANGSTA CITY

By **Teddy Duke**

A DRUG KING AND HIS DIAMOND I & II III

A DOPEMAN'S RICHES

By Nicole Goosby

TRAPHOUSE KING **I II & III**

By **Hood Rich**

LIPSTICK KILLAH **I, II**

CRIME OF PASSION

By **Mimi**

STEADY MOBBN'

By **Marcellus Allen**

WHO SHOT YA **I, II**

Renta

BOOKS BY LDP'S CEO, CA$H

TRUST IN NO MAN

TRUST IN NO MAN 2

TRUST IN NO MAN 3

BONDED BY BLOOD

SHORTY GOT A THUG

THUGS CRY

THUGS CRY 2

THUGS CRY 3

TRUST NO BITCH

TRUST NO BITCH 2

TRUST NO BITCH 3

TIL MY CASKET DROPS

RESTRAINING ORDER

RESTRAINING ORDER 2

IN LOVE WITH A CONVICT

Coming Soon

BONDED BY BLOOD 2

BOW DOWN TO MY GANGSTA

MEESHA